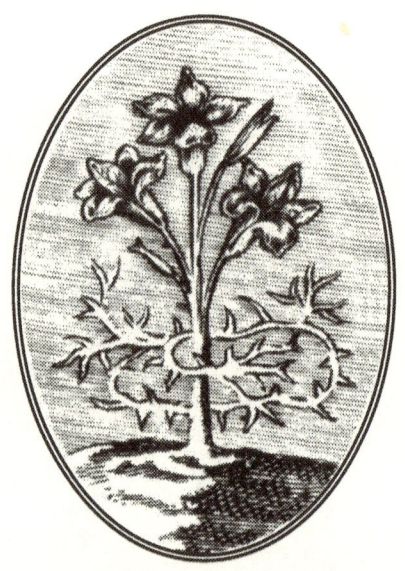

Sicut lilium inter spinas sic amica mea inter filias

On The Cover: We use the symbol of the "lily among the thorns" from Song of Solomon 2:2 to represent the Baptist History Series. The Latin, *Sicut lilium inter spinas sic amica mea inter filias*, translates, "As the lily among thorns, so is my love among the daughters."

Ill Newes

From

NEW-ENGLAND

JOHN CLARKE
1609-1676

This picture hangs in the Redwood Library in Newport, Rhode Island. It has been traditionally considered an authentic portrait of Dr. John Clarke.

ILL NEWES

FROM

NEW-ENGLAND:

OR

A Narative of *New-Englands*

PERSECUTION.

WHERIN IS DECLARED

That while old *England* is becoming new,
New-England is become Old.

Also four Proposals to the Honoured Parliament and
Councel of State, touching the way to *Propagate
the Gospel of Christ* (with small charge
and great safety) both in Old
England and New.

Also four conclusions touching the faith and order of the
Gospel of Christ out of his last Will and
Testament, confirmed and justified.

By JOHN CLARKE Physician of Rhode Island in *America*.

Revel. 2.25. Hold fast till I come.
3.11. Behold I come quickly
22.20. Amen, even so come Lord Jesus.

LONDON,

Printed by *Henry Hills* living in *Fleet-Yard* next door to the *Rose*
and *Crown*, in the year 1652.

The Baptist Standard Bearer, Inc.

NUMBER ONE IRON OAKS DRIVE • PARIS, ARKANSAS 72855

Thou hast given a *standard* to them that fear thee;
that it may be displayed because of the truth.
-- Psalm 60:4

Reprinted
by

THE BAPTIST STANDARD BEARER, INC.
No. 1 Iron Oaks Drive
Paris, Arkansas 72855
(501) 963-3831

THE WALDENSIAN EMBLEM
lux lucet in tenebris
"The Light Shineth in the Darkness"

ISBN #1-57978-827-0

TABLE OF CONTENTS

Baptist History Series Logo....................................page ii

John Clarke Picture...page iv

Complete Title..page v

Baptist Standard Bearer Logo...............................page vi

Table of Contents...page 1

PART 1 — The Epistle Dedicatory........................page 3

PART 2 — To The Honored Magistry....................page 10

PART 3 — To The Christian Reader......................page 18

PART 4 — Preface to the Main Narrative..............page 22

PART 5 — Main Narrative of the Book.................page 27

About the Author..page 115

For Further Reading...page 119

To the Right Honorable the House of PARLIAMENT, and COUNCEL of STATE for the Commonwealth of ENGLAND, The author humbly craves of that mighty Counseller, that Prince of peace, a large donation of the spirit of Counsell, and of the spirit of courage, with a suitable and happy success for the *Peace, Liberty,* and enlargement of these three *Nations.*

MAY it please you right Honorable, in some of those few vacant hours which it pleaseth the most high (whose rod and staff you are) to afford unto you, from those many, weighty, difficult, and distractfull incombrances, and affairs, that do flow in, and press upon you daily, to cast your eye (at least for recreations sake) upon this Treatise, and the rather, because it contains in it matter of no small concernment, as in it self, so especially to your honoured selves; for in the first part, which is the narrative, you may please to read a tragicall story, wherein I hope your eye will not a litle affect your tender hearts, to see such a discurteous entertainment of strangers, and wayfaring-men that were passing by, and tarried but for a night or two, and that by their neighbours, men professing the fear of the Lord as they also do; who together for liberty of their consciences, and worship of their God, as their hearts were perswaded, long since fled from the persecuting hands of the Lordly *Bishops,* your adversaries and ours, unto those utmost parts of the World, to the extreme hazard of their lives, the wasting of their estates, and upon the point, to the totall loss and deprivation of their neer and deer relations, and the comforts thereof in this their native land; and the rather to see this acted by that sword, that hand, which from your honoured arm they are betrusted

with, and so to see your sword, your power, your hand
misused therein.   In the second part, which is the confirmation of my testimony by the word of God, and testimony of Christ Jesus the Lord, and especially in the later
part thereof: you that count it your greatest honour, and
highest preferment in this world to be servants of Christ
(who is indeed the Lord of Lords, and King of Kings,
whose Sword-bearers you are, as was also that *Cæsar* although he knew it not) you (I say I hope) shall find that
he hath not required such things at your hands, as generally they that have been his Sword-bearers before your
selves have been apt to conceive; and thereupon have
been too deeply engaged in the shedding of much innocent bloud in this Land; being also perswaded thereunto
by their teachers, who to maintain their superstitious, humane, invented religion and worship, for filthy lucres sake,
it being the only curious art, and craft by which they had
their wealth and livings as those of old; not having the
two-edged sword of the Spirit, which is the word of God,
to defend themselves, and to maintain their craft, against
the poor illiterate and despised servants and witnesses of
Jesus Christ, have been forced to call for the sword of
steel, the power of the Magistrate, to help to stop their
mouthes, to cut them off, and so to take them out of their
way, and by casting a mist before their Rulers eyes they
have still perswaded them, That this is their office, and
duty to do, and that hereby they did God best service with
that sword with which they were betrusted, whereas indeed they did but make their sword guilty of the blood of
the innocent; and thus were they taken off from attend-
ing upon the very thing for which this sword was put into
their hands, to attend upon their private, and carnall interests, and so were brought into a double transgression.
By whose erratacs, Right Honourable, I hope the Lord
will teach you to beware, and by giving you a clear dis-
cerning of his mind, and will in these more bright sunne-
shining daies (wherein the Earth begins to be filled with
the knowledge of the Lord as the waters cover the Sea)
will give you to understand that as all power in earth is
given to him, so he to the glory of God his Father, whose
power, and wisdome he is, doth wisely manage the same

by a two fold administration of power suitable to the two
fold state or being of man, whom in the earth, and in the
things thereof he hath appointed Lord; that one may be
called an earthly, and outward administration, which suits
the outward man, and all those outward, and visible things
(in reference unto man) that do belong thereto, as he is
Lord thereof, and is managed by an outward visible sword
of steel, and by a carnall or audible voyce, or word of him,
or them that holds it in their hand, and to an outward
and carnal end, (yet righteous, just, and good, which being diligently attended to tends to the peace, liberty, and
prosperity of a civil State, Nation and Kingdom so far as
it concerns the outward man and visible state thereof;)
which end is the preservation of it self, the whole, and
every particular part, and person, belonging thereunto,
safe in their person, name, and estate from him, or them
that would rise up visibly to oppress, or wrong them in
the same; Thus in the general; and to instance more
particularly, in case by the caution of a wholesome Law,
and just penalty annexed thereunto, which by a carnall
hand or way, is presented to a carnall and visible eye, or
ear, the Oppressour takes not warning, and will not be
deterred from offering violence to the person, name, or
estate of his neighbour, then by this power shall he be
made responsible, and be forced *nolens volens*, so far as he
is able to make it good, and to restore; in case any be
impoverished, or faln to decay in their outward man, and
estates by age, sickness, fire, or by some other way, or
hand of GOD; so far as their present strength extends, by
this power they are to be employed, and where it fails,
to be relieved, and that by an equall, and just levy of
their neighbours estates to be taken also by force in case
there be not so much love, and charity in them towards
their poor distressed neighbours to constrain them thereunto, and by the same way also to maintain it self, and all
other just undertakings that may be presented for the
preservation of the whole. And this in brief is the sum
of that administration of Christs power in earth so far as
it meerly concerns the outward man with respect to others
that may uphold it, or molest it, and is managed by that
sword of steel which in reference unto him is called in

scripture the rod of iron by which he rules the nations,
and breaks them to peeces like a Potters vessel; and with
this administration of his power on Earth (Right Honourable) hath he (who is the Lord of Lords and shall ere long
appear as King and judge of all) betrusted you in these
three Nations, having as a manifest token thereof put into
your hand that iron rod, and to admiration hath strength-
ened and upheld your arm for the subduing, and ordering
of the same.

There is yet besides this, another administration of
Christs power on Earth, which compared with this, may
be truly termed heavenly and spirituall, it being that
which suiteth with, and principally is exercised about
the spirituall, or hidden part of man, to wit, his spirit,
mind, and conscience, which is indeed the most naturall
Lord and commander of the outward, it and all things
belonging thereunto being but naturally subject, and readily obedient, from which very consideration it is, that it is
more safe, and also more honourable, for the powers on
earth to have one thousand souls to be subject to them for
love and conscience sake, than to have ten thousand times
ten thousand bodies seemingly subject, for wrath sake,
and for fear of revenge; this spirit and great commander
in man, is such a sparkling beam, from the Father of
lights, and spirits, that it cannot be lorded over, commanded, or forced, either by men, devils, or angels, but
onely leaving its first station, wherein it came so neer to
the light and glory of God, it is now caused to possess
death and darkness, and by that means is in a capacity by
men and devils to be deceived, and so by perswasion to be
mis-led. This spirituall administration of Christs power
in and over the spirits and consciences of men, as it extends to all the inward and hidden motions and actings of
the mind, so to all the outward manifestations of its powerfull commands in the outward man, in reference unto
God, and especially unto such as appertain to the visible
worship and service of God, who hath declared himself to
be a Spirit, and will be worshipped in spirit and in truth,
and seeks such, and onely such to worship him: This spirituall administration so far as it concerns the outward man,
is managed not by a sword of steel (which cannot come

neer or touch the spirit or mind of man) but by the sword
that proceeds out of the mouth of his servants, the word
of truth, and especially as to the efficacy, and to the inward man, by the two-edged sword of the Spirit, that spirituall law and light with which these candles of the Lord
are enlightned, and that by himself, who is that light *that
enlightneth every man that comes into the world ;* and this
spirituall administration of Christs power on earth in and
over the spirits, minds, and consciences of the sons of men,
and also over the outward man as to worship meerly, is
committed into the hands of the Spirit of Christ, who is
his *vice-roy* here on earth, and is only able to deal with
spirits by way of convincing, converting, transforming,
and as it were a-new creating of them, and so to translate
them out of the Kingdome of darkness, in which they are
by nature, into the glorious liberty of the Saints in light.
Who is pleased also to make use of the mouths of his servants, and through them, as empty reeds, and crooked
rams-hornes, to overturn the spirits, and spirituall strong
holds of men and devils, and by them to convict, avenge,
and execute the sentence written, which upon such as
manifest the enmity that is in their minds in the highest
degree even against the holy Spirit himself (the only sin
unpardonable (for all other sin and blasphemy shall be
forgiven) I say the written sentence that is to be executed
upon such) is *anathema maranatha,* that is, accursed with
this intimation, *our Lord cometh,* leaving them untill he
meet with them ; and otherwise than thus the servants of
Christ cannot proceed, having express command not to
strive, but to be *patient, apt to teach,* in meekness instructing those that oppose themselves, & to wait if God at
any time wil give them repentance to the acknowledgement of the truth ; Thus if it please the Father of lights
to give you (Right Honorable) to distinguish between
these two administrations of Christ's power here on earth,
and to leave that part to himself in the hand of his Spirit,
which cannot be conferred on others, nor yet rightly managed but by the *two-edged sword of that Spirit,* and wholly
give up your selves to improve that part which belongs
unto, and well suits with that sword which you are now
betrusted with, it will much conduce to his glory, your

own praise, and the peace and settlement of these three Nations, over which the Lord hath set you.

And whereas Right Honorable, it is in your hearts, to propagate the Gospell of Jesus Christ; the thing is excellent that is in your hearts, and I hope the way to effect it is before you, which is, sith the Lord of hoasts hath said, that works of this nature are carried on, *not by might, nor by power, but by his Spirit,* therefore to give way to his Spirit for the effecting thereof: and to this end I humbly propose, that your way to further this glorious design, as to the might and power this Lord of Hoasts hath betrusted you with, is

1. Not so much as to touch his Anointed, and to do his Prophets no harm, their ointment being the Spirit of prophecy, and this Spirit of prophecy the testimony and witness of the Gospel of Jesus. And

2. As obedient and dutifull servants to that Lord of Lords, to suffer the *Tares* (which being by the adversary sown after the *Wheat,* must needs be ment, erronious, hereticall, and antichristian persons professing the Gospel, I say to let these *tares*) alone in that part of the field, or world, over which the great Lord of the harvest hath placed your Honors; sith it is his pleasure they shall there remain to the time of the harvest, being the end of the world, and that out of his tender respect to the *Wheat,* lest in plucking up the *tares* (though evidently discerned by his servants) the *Wheat* should be rooted up also. And

3. To the same end not to give your sword, or power to the beast nor yet to suffer your power, neither in these three nations, nor yet in any forreign part of the world to be so misused by any to whom 'tis committed, as by vertue thereof out of an ignorant zeal, and blind devotion, pretending to pluck up the tares (which yet is contrary to the express mind of the Lord) to root up the wheat also.

4. To countenance and incourage (as through God's mercifull hand on your hearts in some measure you do) such as are faithful, and upright in the land, by this means shall a wide and effectual door be opened, and so shall the word of the Lord, which is the Gospel of Christ go forth, run and be glorifyed through all those parts of the world that acknowledge your power, and that which

is of God shall stand, encrease and be propagated, and that which is not of God shall fall, decay, and come to nothing. Thus shall you also accomplish the words of the Prophets of old, in becoming *nursing fathers unto the servants, and children of God,* who under you shall lead a peaceable, and quiet life in all godliness, and honesty, and shall be greatly obliged to improve their interest in the father of mercies by their presenting to him constant and earnest petitions, supplications, intercessions, and giving of thanks on your behalf. And for the further-ance of those worthy thoughts of your hearts, they shall not cease to preach, and declare to great, and small what they have seen, and felt, and heard touching the Gospel of Christ, and to pray the lord of the harvest to send forth faithful and painful labourers into his harvest; which is also the constant, hearty, and earnest request of

Your humble and faithful

Subject,

JOHN CLARK.

To the Honored Magistracy, the Presbytery, *and their dependency in the* Mathatusets *Colony in* New-England, *The Author wisheth repentance to the acknowledgement of the truth as it is in Jesus Christ.*

HOnored Friends, for so without scruple or dissimulation can I call you ; some of you I honor for your parts, others for your places sake, and both for many good things I see in you, and for evils reformed by you ; I call you friends, for my love to you (in truth) is unfained, neither are there (I bless the Lord notwithstanding the discurteous usage which I and my friends received from you) any evill thoughts in my heart towards you, because I judge you were put upon what you did by a zeal (I would not think, unto private or carnall interests but) towards God, thinking thereby to do him service ; although I confidently believe, and therefore boldly do affirm that his soul abhors it ; And that I may deal plainly with you as a friend, I will tell you what in my heart I think and judge, that such a zeal of God is not according to true knowledge, or knowledge of the truth as it is in Jesus Christ, which would soon take you off, and free you from that soul murdering, and blood thirsty lie. I hope you will not be offended to see this Narrative brought forth into the publick view, it being upon the point forst from me by your friends and agent here, seeing also the matter, which is contained therein is of no less than of publick concernment, was not done in a corner, is the fruit of your zeal, and that wherein I suppose you glory and count your selves herein a worthy pattern for all that fear the Lord, to follow you, and with all their might to be conformed to ; which if a truth, I then save

you a labour, and further your design, yea I publish your
praise, and glory, but my own disgrace and shame; but
if a mistake, and falsehood, I shall then hereby give occasion unto your faithful friends (whose words may be of
more prevailing power, and force than mine, through
prejudice for present, are like to be) to tell you friendly,
and yet plainly, that you do but glory in your shame, so
that the time may come, if so be the will of God, that
you may smite upon your thigh, and say within yourselves, what fruit had we then of those things, whereof
we are now ashamed; neither let it be offensive to your
spirits to see my testimony for which thing sake among
you we were shamefully entreated, being also strangers to
you and belonging to another jurisdiction where and by
whose means divers of you, and yours, and such as have
been of chiefest note, and most highly esteemed by you,
have enjoyed curtesies with far greater liberties in point
of conscience no man gainsaying: let it not offend I say
to see this testimony when none of you (upon the oft repeated motion) would come forth to oppose it, then to be
made yet more publick, and by the word of God, and testimony of Christ Jesus the Lord to be brought forth into
the open view of all, confirmed and justifyed: neither take
it ill that sith I could not with freedom, and upon equal
terms speak with you, and discuss these points for which
we have been sentenced, that then I have made bold to
write unto you some few lines, that thereby I might re-
mind you (least you let it slip) that we were brought before you as by a hand from beneath, so not without a
speciall, and good hand from above, and that to be a testimony against you in these two weighty particulars; first
to bear testimony against your standing with respect to
the worship of God appointed by Christ, which in plain
terms (for it is not now a time to dissemble seeing the
Lord is at hand) is false, and evil, not the order of the
Gospel of Christ as you pretend, and therefore disorder,
confusion, and that, which in Scripture language is called
Babel; And secondly to bear testimony, or witness against
that way by which you maintain it, which being chiefly
as it appears by carnal weapons, which cannot reach to
the heart or spirit of a man, which is the principal part,

and upon the point the whole in the worship of God, without which there is no acceptance with him, this I say must needs also be fals, but yet far worse, it being no way appointed, or approved of Christ, nor yet groundedly expected or practised by Christians who first trusted in Christ, and therefore upon due examination will prove most unchristian, yea Antichristian; I shall use but these two arguments in this place to convince you, The first whereof standeth thus.

That order, and way to mantain it which neither hath precept from Christ, and his Apostles in his last will and testament, nor yet president, or example among those that first trusted in Christ, that order cannot be the order of the Gospel of Christ, nor that way his way to maintain it.

But the order which you call the order of the Gospel of Christ, and the way which you say is his way to maintain it, hath neither precept, nor president in his last will and testament.

The first proposition I suppose none of you can deny, unless you can find a later than that which is called his last will and testament, and as for the second the truth thereof, will as easily appear if you bring your order, and way to maintain it to the precept of Christ, and practise of those that first trusted in him; and first for your order, what precept from Christ, or practise among those that first trusted in him have you for baptizing of infants (who are declared to be but flesh and by nature the Children of wrat᠂ one as well as another:) for rantising and sprinkling them, and not baptizing or dipping them; for accepting such as were sprinkled with superstitious hallowed water, and by the hand of as superstitious consecrated a ministery of Antichrist, and for receiving of such as are sprinkled by yourselves to the ordinance of Baptism as you call it, but yet to deny them communion in the Apostles doctrine, and in breaking of bread: And if you cannot find either precept from Christ or his Apostles, or example among those that first trusted in Christ for none of these, then will you be at loss for the rest, and neither, find precept or president for your joining together, or for your imitation of those that first trusted in him in their ministery of continuance together in the Apostles doctrine and fellowship and breaking of bread, and prayer. And touching your way to maintain it, what have you a precept and president in the last will and testament of Christ for such a gathering together with respect to the order of the Gospell of Christ in the name, and by the leave of the Magistrate, so as to make it a thing unlawful for the servants of Christ to do it, without him, by the civil sword to correct errour, heresies, and all false worships, to constrain all Church-members, and such also as are without (and so cannot but by you be looked upon to be without faith, without which it is impossible to please God) outwardly and hypocritically to conform to your worship, or to restrain them in like manner outwardly and hypocritically from enjoying their own, when according to that rule (to which is annexed the promise of peace to such as walk thereby) the greatest Apostacies and Blasphemies (that unpardonable sin itself not excepted) were but punished with a delivery of the person that was guilty thereof unto Satan the God of this world, that he might learn not to blaspheme the God of heaven, and so to leave him to the coming of the Lord who shall come in flaming fire to render vengeance upon such ; and so much is signified by the word *Anathema Maranatha.* And I pray consider whether this be not to place the Magistrate *too* high, **or** too low ; too high in case you make him the chief, and upon the point the only Judge in spiritual things (such as appertain to the mystery of godliness that is so great, and such as belong to the mystery of the Kingdome of Christ, that is so wonderful) so as to judge, and determine what is truth, and what is error and heresie, what is the right way of the worship of God who being a spirit hath declared that he will be worshipped in spirit, and in truth, and what is not ; who are the worshippers he seeks for, and who are such as his soul abhors? and again too low in case you make him but the executioner only of other mens judgements; which indeed is the ordinary practise. And so I have done with the first argument; the second stands thus.

2. *Arg.* That order, and way to maintain it which is not only different from, but contrary unto the precept of Christ in his last will and testament, and the practise of

Christians that first trusted in him, that order cannot be
the order of the Gospel of Christ, nor that way his way to
maintain it. But the order which you call the order of
the Gospel of Christ, and the way which you say is his
way to maintain it, is not only different from but contrary
unto the precept of Christ, and the practise of Christians
that first trusted in him.

The first proposition is undeniable, and the second will
easily appear to be true if your order, and that way by
which you seek to maintain it be brought to and compared with the precept of Christ, and his Apostles, and
the example of those churches that first trusted in him;
and first compare but your order with either precept, or
president; and it will evidently appear not only to be differing from, but contrary unto the order of the Gospel of
Christ: for according to the precept of Christ every creature to whom the Gospel was to be preached was by the
preaching thereof to be made a disciple before he was to
be baptized, and then being so made, and baptized he was
to be taught to observe all things which Christ had commanded, which was in reference to a sober, righteous, and
godly conversation in the order of his house, according to
which precept was the practise of those that first trusted
in him, for they, and they only that gladly received the
word of salvation by Jesus Christ were baptized, *Acts* 2
and they, and all they that were baptized were joined
without the leave of the Magistrate, and continued together steadfastly in the Apostles doctrine; and in fellowship, and breaking of bread and prayer: but your joining
together not at the command of the Lord, but by the leave
of the Magistrate, and your continuing together in imitation of the first Churches, and appointing a ministery before your selves be baptized, and so visibly planted into
the death of Christ as they were; and your administring
baptism (as you call it) to such as are not the true subjects thereof before they are taught, or made disciples;
and after a false manner, viz. by sprinkling, which no
way resembles the death, burial, or resurrection of Jesus
Christ, being that which his baptisme is appointed to do;
and your admitting some unto baptism (as you own it)
which you refuse to admit unto breaking of bread, and

your receiving such to breaking of bread, which yet were
never baptized with the baptism appointed by Jesus Christ
the Lord; and your shutting out the exercise of the gift
of prophecying, which in the Church of Christ doth ad-
mirably tend to edification; and your introducing a mixt
confused way of singing which fills the ear rather with a
loud sound of words, than the heart with any thing that
is truly edifying, all which is not only differing from, but
contrary unto both precept, and president, and so cannot
be the order of the Gospel of Christ, and therefore is no
better than disorder, confusion, and a part of that which
in Scripture language is called Babell. And compare that
way by which you maintain it, either with the precept of
Christ or with the president of primitive Christians and it
will as evidently appear not only to be different from, but
contrary unto them both; for first the precept of Christ
was to learn of him who was meek and lowly, and to expect trouble, and persecution from others, and not to persecute, neither to force the Jews that would not follow
him, nor yet to fire the Samaritans that would not receive
him, yea he expressely commands his Servants to let the
tares alone with the wheat, and suffers no small inconvenience thereby to avoid a greater, and further declares
that the servant of the lord must not strive, but be gentle
unto all men, apt to teach (not to strike) patient, in meekness instructing those that oppose themselves, if God peradventure will give them repentance to the acknowledgement of the truth that they may recover themselves out
of the snare of the devil who are taken captive by him at
his will; according to which precepts of Christ we find
the primitive Christians were meek, and gentle, and yet
able by sound doctrine both to exhort, and convince the
gainsayers, who called not for carnall weapons to mannage
their warfare, but declared their weapons were mighty
through God, and either by the word and a good conversation wonne men to the acknowledgement of the truth
as it is in Jesus, or else left them without excuse together
with the world, unto the judgement of the great day of
the Lord; but now all men may see that your way is
not only different from, but contrary unto this precept of
Christ and president of Christians, and therefore cannot

be esteemed any better than unchristian, yet Antichristian.

Let not your adversary and mine (Dear Countreymen) fill your hearts with indignation, and thoughts of revenge against him, who in a faithful discharge of his conscience both towards God, and you, have made bold to deal plainly with you, least my God to whom vengeance belongs, repay it upon you, and smite you with blindness of mind, and hardness of heart that cannot repent, but rather set before your eyes that memorable practice, and worthy pattern of those noble Bereans, and (laying profits, honor and prejudice aside if it be possible) peruse my testimony, and search the scriptures diligently to see whether the things contained therein be so or no; if you find them so, viz. confirmed, and justifyed by the word of God, and by the testimony of Christ Jesus the Lord, then consider, not I but the Lord from heaven calls upon you to break off your sins by repentance, and let me hereby give you warning to take heed that you dispise not him that speaketh from heaven. As touching the wrong and injury done to us, you having thereby much more wronged your own souls in transgressing the very law, and light of Nations, doing as you would not be done unto, it is in my heart to pitty you rather, and to petition my Lord in heaven not to lay this sin to your charge, than to complain against you, or to petition your lords and ours here on earth for justice herein; no, no, we have better learned Christ than so, having also given up our hearts to be led by his spirit; and to walk in his steps, who when he was reviled, reviled not again, when he suffered, he threatned not, but committed his case to him that judgeth righteously, and who knowes but that the spirit of judgement, and the spirit of burning, hath been, or may be ere long in your hearts, whereby you may be made affectedly sensible, that the cause is the same, or very little differing from this.

A poor innocent traveller passeth along the countrey upon his occasions: a man having strength in his arm findeth him, frames himself offended with him for no cause he hath given him, and because he cannot draw him unto his party, either to rob, or to kill, or to say amen to his practises, he therefore binds him, and casts him into a pit, and declares himself resolute there to keep him, till he hath his blood, unless he will deliver him his purse; the man either hath not a purse about him, or a heart to deliver it; and being unwilling either to part with his blood, or that the other should be so deeply guilty in taking it from him, he meekly, and earnestly thrice moveth the strong man for a discourse, and humbly entreats him that he would not seek by the strenth of his arme, but by the force of some arguments to convince his understanding, and conscience, and so to draw him (as a man) to his party, but the strong man delaies him, and so puts him off; whereupon a good tender hearted Samaritan passing by, and perceiving how the case stood, and that the strong man would have his purse, or his blood without any dispute, being moved with compassion to redeem this innocent blood from the hand of the strong man he delivers him his own purse, and so the man is released. Take it not ill that I have used so much plainess of speech, for my studie is now to speak plainly, and neither flatteringly nor invectively: and to use plain dealing with all men, although I verifie the Proverb, and die a begger; for as I told some of your selves (and that in publick) I abhor dissimulation, neither can I account him a wise man who doth not hate dissembling, or that doth love to dissemble; and therefore saith *Solomon* rebuke a wise man and he will love thee, &c. and *David* the King saith on this wise, let the righteous smite me and it shall be a precious balm; I know instruction is grievous to him that is out of the way, but what saith the wise man, he that hateth instruction shall die. Consider I pray what hath been spoken, and turn not away your eye, nor your ear, nor your heart from instruction, least that which was said by the prophet of old *Isa.* 9. 14, 15, 16, be in you verified, which to prevent is the humble and earnest request unto the fathers of mercies of

         Your loving friend and
                Countreyman
            JOHN CLARK.

To the true Christian Reader.

THOU maist herein (Christian Reader) see, and peruse thy destiny in this present evill world (which seems in a great measure to be subjected unto devils) through which thou art to pass unto that purchased possession, and promised inheritance of the Saints in light, which is in that better world, which is not subjected unto Angels, but unto the Sonne of God himself; thou maist herein also observe, and take notice of the hand by whom from thy heavenly father thou art to receive that bitter cup, which he drunk off when he was here below; for thy sake chiefly was this treatise brought forth into the publick view; I hope not to discourage thee, but to strengthen thine heart, that thou mightest not fear any of those things, which thou shalt suffer, either from men or devils for thy testimony, that Jesus is the Christ (it being that which will shortly appear the only prevailing, and victorious truth in all the world): for herein shalt thou also see that worthy saying lively accomplished; If ye suffer for the name of Christ blessed are ye, for the spirit of the Lord, and of glory resteth upon you; thou hast a worthy name called on thee. My hearts desire, and prayer to God on thy behalf, therefore is that thou maist enjoy such a plentifull pouring forth of that holy spirit into thine heart, that thereby thou maist be inabled to walk worthy of it, and having so bright a beam of the Fathers glory in thy soul, it may so shine forth before the sons of men, that they seeing thy good works may have cause administered to glorify our father, which is in heaven; It is not words now Christian, (although they were spoken with tongues of men and Angels) when that worthy name is every where well spoken of, but faith that works by love, and love by works that will distinguish a heady from a hearty Christian. Say not in thine heart that Christs Comands are low, and his appointments carnall, legal injunctions, and at the best, but meat for babes; least hereby thine heart be declared to be vainly puft up in thy carnall or fleshly mind, and to have too low, and carnall conceits of Christ himself, who is the injoyner, appointer, and commander thereof, and shall ere long appear as Judge, yea least hereby thou be declared ignorant, or at the best forgetful of this one thing, that it is the great design of God in Christ as to glorifie himself to admiration in poor sinful flesh, so whilest he doth it to hide pride from man, and therefore as he hath chosen not many wise, mighty, nor noble of this world, but the foolish, weak, base, despised nothings thereof, so hath he suited his commands, and appointments thereunto, and intends through these foolish things so to cause his wisdome to shine forth as thereby to confound the wise; through these weak things so to cause his power to appear, as thereby to confound the things that are mighty; and through these base dispised things that are not, to bring to nought those noble, glorious, and excellent things of the world that are; Thou mayst herein see (gentle Reader) that I have rather chosen to bear witness to the faith, and order of our Lord, and to shew unto the world, but especially unto thee, what is the mind of Christ in this time of his absence as to faith, and obedience, to shew I say rather what is truth, which is but one, than to bear witness against the ly, which is so various, knowing that the truth once established shall discover the falshood, and light breaking forth shall scatter the darkness. And whilest I lead thee forth to seek him whom thy soul loveth, and longeth after, who is also thy joy, and thy Crown; while I lead thee I say by the footsteps of those flocks that first trusted in Christ, and were fed by such pastors according to his own heart, as he gave them, God forbid that thou shouldst be as one that wilt turn aside by the flocks of his companions, and shouldst be found remaining either on the left side in a visible way of worship in deed, but such as was neither appointed by Christ, nor yet practised by them who first trusted in him, or on the right in no visible way of worship, or order at all, either pretending that the outward court is given to the Gentiles, and the holy City is by them to be troden under foot; that the Church

of Christ is now in the wilderness, and the time of its
recovery is not yet, or else pretending that God is a spirit,
and so will in spirit be worshipped, and not in this place
or that, in this way or that.   Well if thou beest in these
waies misled I can no longer forbear in tenderness of
spirit, and compassionate bowels of love to stretch forth a
helping hand thereby to try whether it be the good pleasure of God at this time to drop down a word of light, and
life, and power into thine heart, that thou mayest be
thereby awakened, and quickned to be still saying within
thy soul; Lord what wilt thou have me to do? so shalt
thou hear such a saying as this, *Come out from among
them (Oh my people) and be ye separate from them, and
touch no unsanctifyed thing, and I will receive you, and be
a father unto you, and ye shall be my sons, and daughters,*
saith the Lord God Almighty, and also such a saying as
this, *Blessed are they that do his commands for they have
right to the tree of life, and shall enter in through those
gates of pearl into that glorious City;* Rev. 22. 14. and
know that these are the commandments of *Jesus* sci. *As ye
have received Christ Jesus the Lord, so walk ye in him;
and behold I come quickly, hold that fast which thou hast,
yea hold fast till I come;*   And such as may be under the
later disceptions let me intreat thee to ponder these words
in thine heart sci. That prophecies although marvelous
plain, and easy to be understood, cannot warrant a pure
conscience to neglect, much less to cast off the commandments and appointments of Jesus, neither can the spirit
of Christ direct or incourage the heart of a Christian to
cast off his lordship; no, no, the spirit of Christ is hereby
distinguished from that of Antichrist, in that he shall un-
fainedly confess that Jesus is the Christ, and that this
Christ Jesus is come in the flesh, and when he is come
according to promise into the heart of a Christian, he
shall not speak of himself, but as a messenger his office is
to glorifie Christ by taking of him, and his, and shewing
it unto, yea writing it in the heart of a Christian, so that
I dare boldly say, there is none for the exaltation of Christ
Jesus the lord according to his last will and testament,
and for the nourishing a lively hope in the heart of a
Christian concerning his glorious return, I say there is

none to that holy spirit of promise, who being also the spirit of truth, shall guide the souls of the Saints to worship the father, as in spirit, so likewise in truth ; and therefore that spirit that speaks of himself, and is so far from taking of Christs to exalt, and gloryfie him according as he hath foretold and his father intended, that he takes from Christ, laies him low, and diminisheth his glory, that spirit cannot be the spirit of Christ, or that holy spirit of promise ; and forasmuch as the spirit speaketh expressly that in these later daies there shall be seducing spirits that *shall deceive if it were possible the very elect of God,* whose incounter will not be so much with flesh and blood, but with wicked spirits in high places, let me therefore exhort thee in the words of that beloved disciple of Christ ; *beleive not every spirit, but try the spirits ;* and that by this rule, *whether they be of God or no,* bring them to the wholsome words of the holy Apostles, Prophets, and son of God ; *ye erre* (saith Christ) *not knowing the scriptures, and the power of God ;* let it be thy care (Christian) therefore to search the Scriptures, and therein to wait for the power and glory of the spirit of God. And look to thy spirit for as immediately before Christs appearing in flesh, Satan in a large measure possessed the bodies of men, that by his casting them out, his power in flesh might appear ; So before his coming again in glory I have grounds to expect that the minds and spirits of men shall be strongly possessed ; and that as this fundamentall conclusion, Thou art Jesus the son of the living God, shall be improved to the utmost by the holy Spirit of Christ in the hearts and lives of the sons and daughters of God, so shall the same conclusion be improved to the utmost by way of a bewitching deception in the hearts and lives of the sons of men by the spirit of Antichrist, which mystery being brought to the height, then shall Christ Jesus consume him with the spirit of his mouth, and shall destroy him with the brightness of his coming. Therefore (Christian) stand thou upon thy watch, and know, that if Christ be formed in thee, thou canst not but be transformed by him, and the best form that thou canst be found in when thy Lord shall appear, will be in that form, and so doing, as he hath appointed,

walking wisely and in peace toward all men. Consider
what hath been spoken to thee, and the God of truth and
peace give thee to understand and do his will; which is
the constant and earnest supplication and prayer of

thine in Christ Jesus

JOHN CLARK.

A brief discourse touching New England, *as to the matter
in hand, and to that part of it,* sci. Rode Iland, *where
my residence is, together with the occasion of my going
out with others from the* Mathatusets *Bay, and the many
providentiall occurrences that directed us thereto, and
pitched us thereon.*
As also the Contents of the whole Treatise.

NEw *England* is a name (as is generally known) that
was, and still is, call'd upon that place in reference
to Old; yet not so much because it is peopled, and planted from thence, for so are many other Plantations of the
English in those Western parts; but because it resembles
the same, as the daughter the mother. It resembles it in
the climate, in the times and seasons of the year, in the
fruits which the land naturally produceth, in the fouls,
and the fish that are there in abundance. It resembles it
in their politicall affairs; for their governments, laws,
Courts, Officers, are in a great measure the same, and so
are the names of their towns, and Counties; and in point
of good husbandry, that wᵗʰ is raised and produced in
New *England*, more substantiall, and whether it be for
food or raiment it is the same with that which is here
produced in Old. It is a place (in the largest acceptation) that contains in it all the Plantations of the English
upon that coast of *America* that lie between the *Dutch*
Plantation on the West, and the *French* on the East; and
extends it self upon the Sea coast above one hundred
leagues. In it is contained the four Colonies, which call
themselves the united Colonies. The Colony called by
the name of the *Province of Providence Plantations*, lying on the South and South-East thereof, and two or three
more lying on the East or North-East, in *Agamenticus,
Saco, Casco-Bay*, and *Pemaquid*, where is that treasure of

Masts for Ships. The names of the united Colonies are these, in point of precedency first *Mathatusets*, &c. but in point of antiquity first *Plymouth*, then the *Mathatusets*, then *Conectecot*, and last *Quinipiuck*. The chief Towns of these Colonies, and seats of their Government are these, *Boston* of the *Mathatusets*, *Plymouth* of *Plymouth*, *Hereford* of *Conectecot*, and of *Quinipiuck New-Haven.*

Now as the name *New England* in the largest and truest acceptation extends to all the Plantations of the English between the *French* and the *Dutch*, so in a scanty and improper acceptance of the word (especially when it makes for advantage) it is taken for these four united Colonies, by reason of the precedency they have of others, and for the same cause, and upon the point as well, it may be taken for the *Mathatusets* and the Town of *Boston* therein.

When I speak of *New England*, understand it of that part which hath got the precedency (by reason of shipping) and start of the rest, *sci.* the *Mathatusets*, as both in my Epistle and Narrative is plain to be seen, which I have here also inserted for fear of mistake.

In the Colony of *Providence Plantations* in point of antiquity the Town of *Providence* is chief, but in point of precedency *Rode-Iland* excels. This Iland lieth in the *Narraganset Bay*, being 14 or 15 miles long, and in breadth between 4 and 5 miles at the broadest; It began to be planted by the *English* in the beginning of the year 39. [36] and by this hand of providence. In the year 37 I left my native land, and in the ninth moneth of the same, I (through mercy) arived at *Boston*, I was no sooner on shore, but there appeared to me differences among them touching the Covenants, and in point of evidencing a mans good estate, some prest hard for the Covenant of works, and for sanctification to be the first and chief evidence, others prest as hard for the Covenant of grace that was established upon better promises, and for the evidence of the Spirit, as that which is a more certain, constant, and satisfactory witness. I thought it not strange to see men differ about matters of Heaven, for I expect no less upon Earth: But to see that they were not able so to bear each with other in their different understandings and consciences, as in those utmost parts of the World to live peaceably together, whereupon I moved the latter, for as much as the land was before us and wide enough, with the profer of *Abraham* to *Lot*, and for peace sake, to turn aside to the right hand, or to the left: The motion was readily accepted, and I was requested wth some others to seek out a place, which accordingly I was ready to do; and thereupon by reason of the suffocating heat of the Summer before, I went to the North to be somewhat cooler, but the Winter following proved so cold, that we were forced in the Spring to make towards the South; so having sought the Lord for direction, we all agreed that while our vessel was passing about a large and dangerous Cape, we would cross over by land, having *Long Iland* and *Delaware-Bay* in our eie for the place of our residence; so to a town called *Providence* we came, which was begun by one M. *Roger Williams* (who for matter of conscience had not long before been exiled from the former jurisdiction) by whom we were courteously and lovingly received, and with whom we advised about our design; he readily presented two places before us in the same *Naragansets Bay*, the one upon the main called *Sowwames*, the other called then *Acquedneck*, now *Rode-Iland ;* we enquired whether they would fall in any other Patent, for our resolution was to go out of them all; he told us (to be brief) that the way to know that, was to have recourse unto *Plymouth ;* so our Vessell as yet not being come about, and we thus blockt up, the company determined to send to *Plymouth*, and pitcht upon two others together with myself, requesting also M. *Williams* to go to *Plymouth* to know how the case stood; so we did; and the Magistrates thereof very lovingly gave us a meeting; I then informed them of the cause of our coming unto them, and desired them in a word of truth and faithfulness to inform us whether *Sow-wames* were within their Patent, for we were now on the wing, and were resolved through the help of Christ, to get cleer of all, and be of ourselves, and provided our way were cleer before us, it were all one for us to go further off, as to remain neer at hand; their answer was, that *Sow-wames* was the garden of their Patent, and the flour in the garden; then I told

them we could not desire it; but requested further in
the like word of truth and faithfulness to be informed,
whether they laid claim to the Ilands in the *Naraganset
Bay,* and that in particular called *Acquedneck?* they all
with a cheerfull countenance made us this answer, it was
in their thoughts to have advised us thereto, and if the
provident hand of God should pitch us thereon they
should look upon as free, and as loving neighbours and
friends should be assistant unto us upon the main, &c.
So we humbly thanked them, and returned with that answer: So it pleased the Lord, by moving the hearts of the
natives, even the chiefest thereof, to pitch us thereon, and
by other occurrences of providence, which are too large
here to relate: So that having bought them off to their
full satisfaction, we have possessed the place ever since;
and notwithstanding the different understandings and
consciences amongst us, without interruption we agree to
maintain civil Justice and judgement, neither are there
such outrages committed mongst us as in other parts of
the Country are frequently seen.

The Narrative declares
1. How those three strangers were apprehended, imprisoned, sentenced, and for what.
2. How the motion was made for a publique dispute,
   often repeated and promised, and yet disapointed.
3. How two escaped, and the third was cruelly handled.
4. How two, for taking him but by the hand after his
   punishment, were apprehended, imprisoned, and sentenced to pay forty shillings or be whipped.

In their Testimony laid down in four conclusions, is
opened and proved
In the first, 1. That Jesus is the Christ, [i. e.] the
Anointed Priest, Prophet, and King of Saints. 2. That
Christ is also the Lord of his Church in point of ruling
and ordering them with respect to the worship of God.
In the Second, 1. That Baptism is one of the commandments of Christ, and to continue till he come. 2. That
visible Believers are the proper subjects thereof. 3. That

they are as well to wait for the promise of the Spirit, as for the presence of Christ.

In the Third, That every believer ought to improve his talent both in and out of the Congregation.

In the Fourth, That no servant of Jesus hath any authority from him to force upon others either the faith or order of the Gospel of Christ. Wherin are produced 8 arguments against persecution for case of Conscience.

Ill Newes

From

New-England

A Faithfull and True Relation of the Prosecution of Obediah
Holmes, John Crandall, *and* John Clarke, *meerly for
Conscience towards God, by the Principall Members of
the Church, or Common-wealth of the* Mathatusets *in New-
England, which rules over that part of the World; whereby is shewn their discourteous Entertainment of Strangers,
and how that Spirit by which they are led, would order the
whole World, if either brought under them, or should come
in unto them: Drawn forth by the aforesaid* John Clarke,
*not so much to answer the Importunity of Friends, as to
stop the mouthes,. and slanderous reports of such as are
Enemies to the Cross of Christ. Let him that readeth it
consider, which Church is most like the Church of Christ
(that Prince of Peace, that meek and gentle Lamb, that
came into this World to save Mens lives, not to destroy
them,) the Persecuted, or Persecuting.*

IT came to pass that we three, by the good hand of our
God, came into the *Mathatusets* Bay upon the 16 day
of the 5th Moneth, 51; and upon the 19th of the same,
upon occasion of businesse, we came unto a Town in the
same Bay called *Lin,* where we lodged at a Blind-mans
house neer two miles out of the Town, by name *William
Witter,* who being baptized into Christ waits, as we also
doe, for the Kingdom of God, and the full consolation of
the *Israel* of God: Vpon the 20th day, being the first
day of the week, not having freedom in our Spirits for
want of a clear Call from God to goe unto the Publike
Assemblie to declare there what was the mind, and counsell of God concerning them, I judged it was a thing suitable to consider what the counsell of God was concerning
ourselves; and finding by sad experience, that the hour
of temptation spoken of was coming upon all the World
(in a more eminent way) to try them that are upon the
Earth, I fell upon the consideration of that Word of
Promise, made to those that keep the Word of his Patience, which present thoughts, while in Conscience towards God, and good will unto his Saints, I was impart-

ing to my Companions in the house where I lodged, and
to 4, or 5 Strangers, that came in unexpected after I had
begun, opening, and proving what is meant by the hour
of Temptation, what by the Word of his patience, and
their keeping it, and how he that hath the Key of *David*
(being the Promiser) will keep those that keep the word
of his Patience from the hour of Temptation; while I say
I was yet speaking, there comes into the house where we
were, two Constables, who with their clamorous tongues
made an interruption in my Discourse, and more uncivilly
disturbed us, than the Pursivants of the old *English* Bishops were wont to doe; telling us, that they were come
with Authority from the Magistrate to apprehend us; I
then desired to see the Authority by which they thus proceeded, whereupon they pluckt forth their Warrant, and
one of them with a trembling hand (as conscious he might
have been better imployed) read it to us; The substance
whereof was as followeth.

By virtue hereof, you are required to go to the house
of *William Witter*, and so to search from house to house,
for certain erronious persons, being Strangers, and them
to apprehend, and in safe custody to keep, and to morrow
morning by eight of the Clock to bring before me,

Robert Bridges.

When he had read the Warrant, I told them, Friends,
there shall not be (I trust) the least appearance of a re-
sisting of that Authority by which you come unto us; yet
I tell you, that by virtue hereof you are not so strictly
tyed, but if you please, you may suffer us to make an end
of what we have begun, so may you be Witnesses either
to, or against the Faith, and Order which we hold; to
which they answered they could not; then said we, notwithstanding the Warrant, or any thing therein contained,
you may; neverthelesse, if you are streightened in respect
of your understandings and consciences in point of hearing, doe but withdraw your selves before the door, the
time will not be long; which when they refused, we told
them, then here we are, let our Lord doe with us what he
please: So (although there were that profered to be bound
body and goods for our appearance before Mr. *Bridges* the

next morning, according to the Warrant) they apprehended us, and carried us away to the Ale-house or Ordinary;
where after Dinner one of them said unto us, Gentlemen,
if you be free I will carry you to the Meeting; to whom
was replyed, Friend, had we been free thereunto we had
prevented all this ; Neverthelesse, we are in thy hand, and if
thou wilt carry us to the Meeting, thither will we goo ; to
which he answered, then will I carry you to the Meeting.
To this we replyed, because we perceive thou hast not
long been imployed in thine Office, and that may follow
hereupon which thou expectest not, we will inform thee,
That if thou forcest us unto your Assembly, then shall
we be constrained to declare our selves, that we cannot
hold Communion with them ; the Constable answered,
that is nothing to me, I have not power to command you
to speak, when you come there, or to be silent ; to this I
again replyed, (Friend) know a little further ; Since we
have heard the word of Salvation by Iesus Christ, we
have been taught as those that first trusted in Christ, to
be obedient unto him both by word and deed ; wherefore
if we be forc'd to your Meeting, we shal declare our dissent from you both by word and gesture ; after all this,
when he had consulted with the man of the house, he
told us he would carry us to the Meeting, so to their
Meeting were we brought, while they were at their prayers and uncovered ; and at my first stepping over the
threshold I unveiled my self, civilly saluted them, turned
into the Seat I was appointed to, put on my hat again,
and so sat down, opened my Book, and fell to reading :
hereupon Mr. *Bridges* being troubled, commanded the
Constable to pluck off our hats, which he did, and where
he laid mine, there I let it lye, untill their Prayer, Singing, and Preaching was over ; After this I stood up, and
uttered myself in these words following ; I desire as a
Stranger, if I may, to propose a few things to this Congregation, hoping in the proposall thereof I shall com-
mend myself to your Consciences to be guided by that
wisdom that is from above, which being pure, is also
peaceable, gentle, and easie to be intreated, and therewith
I made a stop, expecting, if the Prince of Peace had been
among them, I should have had a suitable answer of

Peace from them; but no other voice I heard, but of their Pastor, as he is call'd, and their Magistrate; Their Pastor answered by way of Quaery, Whether I was a Member of a Church? &c. Before I could give an answer Mr. *Bridges* spake, saying, if the Congregation please to give you leave, well, if not, I shall require you silence, for, said he, we will have no Objections made against what is delivered, &c. To which I answered, I am not about for present to make Objections against what is delivered, but as by my gesture at my coming into your Assembly I declared my dissent from you, so lest that should prove offensive unto some whom I would not offend, I would now by word of mouth declare the grounds, which are these; First, from the consideration we are Strangers each to other, and so Strangers to each others inward standing with respect to God, and so cannot conjoyn and act in Faith, and what is not of Faith, is Sin: And in the second place, I could not judge that you are gathered together, and walk according to the visible order of our Lord; which when I had declared, Mr. *Bridges* told me I done and spoke that for which I must answer, and so commanded me silence: when their meeting was done, the Officers carryed us again to the Ordinary, where being watched over that night, as Theeves and Robbers, we were the next morning carried before Mr. *Bridges*, who made our *Mittimus*, and sent us to the Prison at *Boston;* The words of the *Mittimus* are these.

To the Keeper of the Prison at *Boston.*

By virtue hereof you are required to take into your custody from the Constable of *Lin*, or his Deputy, the bodies of *Iohn Clark*, *Obediah Holmes*, and *Iohn Crandall*, and them to keep, untill the next County Court to be held at Boston, that they may then and there answer to such complaints as may be alleged against them, for being taken by the Constable at a Private Meeting at *Lin* upon the Lords day, exercising among themselves, to whom divers of the Town repaired, and joyned with them, and that in the time of Publick exercise of the Worship of God; as also for offensively disturbing the peace of the Congregation at their coming into the Publique Meeting

in the time of Prayer in the afternoon, and for saying
and manifesting that the Church of *Lin* was not consti-
tuted according to the order of our Lord, &c. for such
other things as shall be alleged against them, concerning
their seducing and drawing aside of others after their
erroneous judgements and practices, and for suspition of
having their hands in the re-baptizing of one, or more
among us, as also for neglecting or refusing to give in
sufficient security for their appearance at the said Court;
hereof fail not at your perill, 22. 5. 51.

Rob. Bridges.

We being by virtue hereof committed to prison, upon
the 5th. day sevennight after were brought to our tryall;
in the forenoon we were examined, in the afternoon, without producing either accuser, witness, jury, law of God,
or man, we were Sentenced; in our examination the Governour upbraided us with the name of Anabaptists; To
whom I answered, I disown the name, I am neither an
Anabaptist, nor a Pedobaptist, nor a Catabaptist; he told
me in hast I was all; I told him he could not prove us
to be either of them; he said, yes, you have Re-baptized;
I denyed it saying, I have Baptized many, but I never
Re-baptized any; then said he, you deny the former Baptism, and make all our worship a nullity; I told him he
said it; moreover I said unto them (for therefore do I
conceive I was brought before them to be a testimony
against them) If the Testimony which I hold forth be
true, and according to the mind of God, which I un-
doubtedly affirm it is, then it concernes you to look to your
standing. The like to this affirmed the other two; so
after much discourse we were committed again to prison,
and in the afternoon towards night, we were called forth
again, and immediately after the Court was set, my sentence was read, which was as followeth.

The Sentence of Iohn Clarke *of* Road-*Iland.* 31. 5. 51.

Forasmuch as you *Iohn Clarke*, being come into this
Iurisdiction about the 20th. of Iuly, did meet at one
William Witters house at *Lin*, upon the Lords day, and
there did take upon you to Preach to some other of the

Inhabitants of the same Town, and being there taken by the Constable, and coming afterward into the Assembly at *Lin*, did in disrespect of the Ordinances of God and his Worship, keep on your Hat, (the Pastor being then in Prayer) insomuch you would not give reverence in valing your Hat till it was forced off your head, to the disturbance of the Congregation, and professing against the institution of the Church, as not being according to the Gospell of Iesus Christ; And that you the said *Iohn Clarke* did upon the day following meet again at the said *Witters*, and in contempt to Authority, you being then in the custody of the Law, and did there administer the Sacrament of the Supper to one excommunicate person, to another under admonition, and to another that was an Inhabitant of *Lin*, and not in fellowship with any Church; and upon your answer in open Court, you affirmed that you did never Re-baptize any, yet did acknowledge you did Baptize such as were Baptized before, and thereby did necessarily deny the Baptism that was before to be Baptism, the Churches no Churches, and also all other Ordinances, and Ministers, as if all were a Nullity; And also did in the Court deny the lawfullness of Baptizing of Infants, and all this tends to the dishonour of God, the despising the ordinances of God among us, the peace of the Churches, and seducing the Subjects of this Commonwealth from the truth of the Gospel of Jesus Christ, and perverting the strait waies of the Lord, therefore the Court doth fine you 20 pounds to be paid, or sufficient sureties that the said sum shall be paid by the first day of the next Court of Assistants, or else to be well whipt, and that you shall remain in Prison till it be paid, or security given in for it.

　　　　　　　By the Court,　　ENCREASE NOWELL.

　　After my sentence was read, the Sentence of the other two were likewise pronounced; the Sentence of *Obediah Holmes* was to pay by the aforesaid time 30 li. or be well whipt; and the sentence of *Iohn Crandall* was to pay 5 pounds, or be well whipt; this being done, I desired to know whether I might not speak a few things to the Court, to which the Governour replied, your sentence is

past. I told him that which I was to speak was in reference unto a promise that was made us by Mr. *Bridges*
when we were first apprehended, and brought before him;
then said the Governour speak on; When we were at first
apprehended and brought before Mr. *Bridges* (said I) I
said unto him we are Strangers, and Strangers to your
Laws, and may be transgressors of them before we are
aware, we would therefore desire this curtesy of you as
Strangers, that you would shew us the Law by which we
are transgressors: But then no other answer could we
have from him than this, when you come to the Court you
shall know the Law; now we have been before the Court
in the forenoon upon examination, this afternoon we have
heard our Sentence read, yet have we not heard the Law
produced by which we are condemned; we therefore now
desire to see the Law in which our Sentence may be read,
and the rather, because we find in the beginning of your
Laws this provision for the security of your own, and we
hope you are not less regardfull of strangers, *viz.* That no
man shall be molested, but by a Law made by the generall Court, and lawfully published, or in defect of a Law
in a particular case, by the Word of God. When this
was spoken Mr. *Bridges* could easily turn to the Law by
which we might be freed, but none were able to turn to
the Law of God or Man by which we were condemned.
At length the Governour stept up, and told us we had
denyed Infants Baptism, and being somewhat transported
broke forth, and told me I had deserved death, and said,
he would not have such trash brought into their jurisdiction; moreover he said, you go up and down, and secretly
insinuate into those that are weak, but you cannot maintain it before our Ministers, you may try, and discourse
or dispute with them, &c. To this I had much to reply,
but that he commanded the Iaylor to take us away; so
the next morning having so fair an opportunity, I made
a motion to the Court in these words following.

To the Honoured Court Assembled at Boston.

Whereas it pleased this Honoured Court yesterday to
condemn the Faith, and Order which I hold and practise,
and after you had past your Sentence upon me for it, were

pleased to expresse, I could not maintain the same against your Ministers, and thereupon publickly profered me a dispute with them, be pleased by these few lines to understand, I readily accept it, and therefore do desire you would appoint the time when, and the person with whom, in that publick place where I was condemned, I might with freedom, and without molestation of the Civill Power dispute that point publickly where I doubt not by the strength of Christ to make it good out of his last Will and Testament, unto which nothing is to be added, nor from which nothing is to be diminished; thus desiring the Father of Lights to shine forth, and by his power to expel the darkness, I remain,   Your well wisher,

From the Prison this 1. 6. 51.   *John Clarke.*

This motion if granted, I desired it might be subscribed by their Secretaries hand, as an Act of the same Court by which we were condemned.

It was presented on the sixth day, and after much ado upon the last day it was concluded it should be granted, and the disputation should be upon the fifth day following, and so by one of the Magistrates information was given me in prison; upon the second day when their Elders were come together, there was no small stir (as I heard) about the businesse, and afterward about the stating of the Question we should dispute upon; whereupon in the closure of the day the Magistrates commanded the Iaylor to bring me before them into the Chamber, which when he had done, they drew forth the motion, and shewing it to me, asked me if I owned that paper, I answered, yea, they quaeried further, whether I was of the same mind touching a disputation, I told them I had not the least reluctancy in my mind touching the thing, provided my motion might be granted, and the grant subscribed with the Secretaries hand as an act of the same Court by which I was condemned; they answered that was but reasonable, &c. Then they demanded of me what the question was that I would dispute upon, whether I would dispute upon the things contained in my Sentence, and maintain my practice, for, said they, the Court Sentenced you not for your judgement or Conscience, but for matter of fact, and

practice; to which I replyed, you say the Court condemned me for matter of fact, and practice; be it so, but
I say that matter of fact and practice was but the manifestation of my judgement and conscience; and I make
account that man is void of judgement, and conscience,
with respect unto God, that hath not a fact, and practice
suitable thereunto; and for the things contained in my
Sentence, they are rather collections, which the Court was
pleased to make and draw from my words, than my words,
themselves; nevertheless I do not say they were unduly
collected; for in truth, if the Faith and order which I
profess do stand by the word of God, then the Faith and
order which you profess must needs fall to the ground;
and if the way you walk in remain, then the way that I
walk in must vanish away, they cannot both stand together; to which they seem to assent; therefore I told
them, that if they please to grant the motion under the
Secretaries hand, I would draw up the Faith, and order,
which I hold as the sum of that I did deliver in open
Court, into three or four Conclusions, which Conclusions
I will stand by, and defend untill he, whom you shall
appoint, shall by the word of God remove me from them;
in case he shall remove me from them, then the disputation is at an end, but if not, then I desire like liberty by
the word of God to oppose the Faith, and order, which
he and you profess, thereby to try whether I may be an
instrument in the hand of God to remove you from the
same; they told me the motion was very fair, and the
way like unto a disputant, and thereupon concluded in
my hearing, and directed also their speech to me, saying,
because the matter is weighty, and we desire that what
can, may be spoken, when the disputation shall be; therefore would we take a longer time; whereas therefore the
time appointed was the next fift day, by reason of the
commencement, which will be the next week, and the
meeting of the Elders, we must defer it now untill the
fift day come fortnight; and so I told them (to be brief)
I was their prisoner, and should attend their pleasure; so
I returned with my keeper to prison again, drew up the
Conclusions, which I was resolved through the strength
of Christ to stand in defence of, and through the impor-

tunity of one of the Magistrates, the next morning very early, I shewed them to him, having a promise I should have my motion for a dispute granted, under the Secretaries hand.

The Conclusions were as followeth.

The Testimony of *Iohn Clarke* a prisoner of Iesus Christ at *Boston* in the behalf of my Lord, and of his people, is as followeth.

1. I Testifie that Iesus of *Nazareth* whom God hath raised from the dead, is made both *Lord* and *Christ ;* This Iesus I say is the *Christ*, in English, the *Anointed* One, hath a name above every name ; He is the *Anointed Priest*, none to, or with him in point of attonement ; The *Anointed Prophet*, none to him in point of instruction ; The *Anointed King*, who is gone unto his Father for his glorious Kingdom, and shall ere long return again ; and that this Iesus Christ is also *The Lord*, none to or with him by way of Commanding and ordering (with respect to the worship of God) the household of Faith, which being purchased with his Blood as *Priest*, instructed, and nourished by his spirit as *Prophet*, do wait in his appointment as he is the *Lord*, in hope of that glorious Kingdom which shall ere long appear.

2. I Testifie that Baptism, or dipping in Water, is one of the Commandements of this Lord Iesus Christ, and that a visible beleever, or Disciple of Christ Iesus (that is, one that manifesteth repentance towards God, and Faith in Iesus Christ) is the only person that is to be Baptized, or dipped with that visible Baptism, or dipping of Iesus Christ in Water, and also that visible person that is to walk in that visible order of his House, and so to wait for his coming the second time in the form of a *Lord*, and *King* with his glorious Kingdom according to promise, and for his sending down (in the time of his absence) the holy Ghost, or holy Spirit of Promise, and all this according the last Will and Testament of that living Lord, whose Will is not to be added to, or taken from.

3. I Testifie or Witness, that every such believer in Christ Iesus, that waiteth for his appearing, may in point of liberty, yea ought in point of duty to improve that

Talent his Lord hath given unto him, and in the Congregation may either aske for information to himself; or if he can, may speak by way of Prophecie for the edification, exhortation, and comfort of the whole, and out of the Congregation at all times, upon all occasions, and in all places, as far as the jurisdiction of his Lord extends, may, yea ought to walk as a Child of light, justifying wisdom with his ways, and reproving folly with the unfruitfull works thereof, provided all this be shown out of a good conversation, as *Iames* speaks with meekness of wisdom.

4. I Testifie that no such believer, or Servant of Christ Jesus hath any liberty, much less Authority, from his Lord, to smite his fellow servant, nor yet with outward force, or arme of flesh, to constrain, or restrain his Conscience, no nor yet his outward man for Conscience sake, or worship of his God, where injury is not offered to the person, name or estate of others, every man being such as shall appear before the judgment seat of Christ, and must give an account of himself to God, and therefore ought to be fully perswaded in his own mind, for what he undertakes, because he that doubteth is damned if he eat, and so also if he act, because he doth not eat or act in Faith, and what is not of Faith is Sin.

These Conclusions being seen at least by one of the Magistrates, notwithstanding the Message to the prison, answer to my self in the Chamber, promise by him that came for the Conclusions, common report abroad that a disputation was granted, the Court broke up, and did nothing; and the next second day following, a Messenger was sent to the prison from the Magistrate, with a release to the keeper, which having received he speedily put me forth; The words of the release follow.

To the Keeper of the prison.

By Virtue hereof you are to release and set at liberty the Body of Mr. *Iohn Clarke*, and this shall be your discharge for so doing. Given under my hand the 11th. of the 6th. Month, 1651.

WILLIAM HIBBINS.

To be brief, &c.　Vnderstanding that some friends had laid down the Money, although contrary to my Counsell, when formerly at severall times, and by severall persons I was moved thereunto, and perceiving now that the Countries expectation (which was not a little raised) touching a disputation was utterly frustrate, and being sensible that it was an easy matter to lay the blame on me, being a person condemned, and also absent, I drew up the former motion, and added thereunto these words following.

Whereas through the indulgency of tender hearted friends, without my consent, and contrary to my judgment, the Sentence, and Condemnation of the Court at Boston (as is reported) have been fully satisfied on my behalf, and thereupon a Warrant hath been procured by which I am secluded the place of my imprisonment, by reason whereof I see no other call for present but to my habitation, and to those neer relations which God hath given me there, yet lest the cause should hereby suffer, which I profess is Christs, I would hereby signifie, that if yet it shall please the honoured Magistrates, or generall Court of this Colony, to grant my former request under their Secretaries hand, I shall cheerfully imbrace it, and upon your motion shall through the help of God come from the Iland to attend it, and hereunto I have subscribed my name,

11*th.* 6. 51.　　　　　　　　　　　　　　*John Clarke.*

Both these the next morning I delivered to the keeper to deliver to the Magistrates, who were to meet at the Commencement at *Cambridge*, which being accordingly performed it was noised abroad the motion was granted, and the writing was in Mr. *Cottons* hand, who was thereby judged to be the man, and best of all approved of by my self for that same purpose, he being the inventor and supporter of that way, in these parts, wherein they walk, and thereupon I took the thing for granted, and to that purpose wrot to my friends who sent to visit me in prison, but upon the fift day, a little before their Lecture at *Boston*, I received a writing subscribed with five of the Magistrates hands, which when I had perused, and saw that they waved the motion, and instead thereof laid two or

three snares before me, I drew up an Answer to their
Writing, being hopeless of a disputation, desired the
Iaylor to deliver it to the Magistrates, took my leave of
my friends, and so departed to go towards the Iland, hav-
ing ten miles that night to travell. Here followeth their
Writing, and my Answer also.

Mr. John Clarke,
We conceive you have mis-reported the Governours
speech in saying you were challenged to dispute with some
of our Elders, whereas it was plainly exprest, that if you
would confer with any of them, they were able to satisfie
you, neither were you able to maintain your practice to
them by the word of God, all which was intended for your
information, and conviction privately; neither were you
enjoyned to what you then were Counselled unto; nevertheless, if you are forward to dispute, and that you will
move it yourself to the Court, or the Magistrates about
Boston, we shall take order to appoint one who will be
ready to Answer your motion, you keeping close to the
questions to be propounded by your self, and a moderator
shal be appointed also to attend upon that service; &
whereas you desire you might be free in your dispute,
keeping close to the points to be disputed on, without
incurring damage by the Civill Iustice, observing what
hath been before written, it is granted; the day may be
agreed if you yeeld the premisses.

Iohn Indicott, Governour.
Tho. Dudley, Deputy Govern.
Rich. Bellingham.
William Hibbins.
Encrease Nowel.

11th. of the 6th. 1651.

My Answer followeth, superscribed,

To the Honoured Governour of the *Mathatusets*, and the
rest of that Honorable Society, these present.
Worthy Senators,
I Received a writing subscribed with 5 of your hands
by way of answer to a twice-repeated motion of mine before you, which was grounded as I conceive sufficiently
upon the Governours words in open Court; which writing

of yours doth no way answer my expectation, nor yet that motion which I made, and whereas (waving that grounded motion) you are " pleased to intimate, That if I were for- " ward to dispute, and would move it myself to the Court, " or Magistrates about *Boston*, you would appoint one to " answer my motion, &c. Be pleased to understand, That although I am not backward to maintain the Faith, and Order of my Lord the King of Saints, for which I have been Sentenced, yet am I not, in such a way so forward to dispute, or move therein, least inconvenience should thereby arise, I shall rather once more repeat my former motion, which if it shall please the Honoured General Court to accept, and under their Secretaries hand shall grant a free dispute without molestation or interruption, I shall be so well satisfied therewith, that what is past I shall forget, and upon your motion shall attend it; Thus desiring the Father of Mercies not to lay that evill to your charge,

From Prison this   I remain your Well-wisher,
14. 6. 51.   *Iohn Clarke.*

This Answer with the motion for a dispute upon these fair termes the third time repeated, (being a thing also generally desired, and longed for) was (as I said before) by me delivered to the Keeper, and by him presented to the Magistrates, and so to the General Court, yet was there no answer returned : what made the obstruction considering the equity of the Case, the former consent and grant of the Magistrates, and the peoples earnest desire thereof, I know not, neither will I too readily conclude (lest it should savor of prejudice) that it was either an apprehension it would be disgracefull, first to Iudge and Condemn the persons, and afterward to have the matter examined, or else a fear and jealousie lest upon the examination thereof by the word of God (which is a quick & powerful divider asunder of the Soul and Spirit, and of the joynts, & marrow, and a discerner of the thoughts and intents of the heart) their standing (in reference to the worship of God) should appear false, and evill, and the way by wch they maintayn the same with a forcing of others thereto, should appear far worse; surely, the stand-

ers by, and such, whose minds are dis-engaged in the
businesse will aptly conclude, and not without probable
grounds, that the utmost they can say for themselves, and
to stop the mouth of him that is contrary minded, lyes in
the Sword and power of the Magistrate, which although
it be a good Ordinance of God in this present evill World,
to restrain the oppressor, and let the oppressed goe free,
and so approved and owned by Christ and all true Christians, in case of wrong and wicked lewdnesse, as *Gallio*
expresseth it, yet was it never appointed by Christ, (to
whom all power, not only in Earth, but also in Heaven,
is committed, and by whom all Earthly powers are to be
judged, in that day in which he shall judge the World in
righteousnesse; I say it was never appointed by Christ)
to inform and rectifie the minds and consciences of men
in the worship of God, in that great mystery of Godli-
nesse, and in those mysticall matters concerning the
Kingdom of Christ, that being a matter that onely belongs to the Holy Spirit of Promise, and to the Sword of
that Spirit, which is the Word (not of man, but) of God,
to effect; much lesse to conform their outward man, contrary to their minds and consciences in the Worship of
God; and therefore that Sword and Power ought to take
heed how they meddle herein (lest they attempt to take
the place, & enter upon the Throne and Kingdom of
Christ) either to force such as be conceived to be true
Worshipers, to the true Worship, and service of God,
for it is written, Not by might, nor by power, but by my
Spirit saith the Lord of Hosts. And again, In the day
of thy power, thy people shall be a willing people; much
lesse to force such as are no Worshipers, or false, to that
Worship which is true, and yet much lesse to force false,
to that which is false, or true, to that which is false; and
hence it is, that although the Kings of the Earth have
been deceived, and through the righteous judgment of
God have given their power to the Beast, to their own
dishonour and detriment, who have improved the same to
bear up the Whore, and to bear down and crush the
Spouse of the Lamb, so that *Babel* hath for a long time
rejoyced, and *Sion* hath mourned; yet when the time
appointed is come, at the voyce of her King *Sion* shall

deliver herself from the Daughter of *Babel*, though all the powers of this World seek to withstand it; neither shall the gates of Hell prevail against it: for it is written concerning those that keep the Commandements of God, and the Testimony of Iesus, that they overcame him (scil. that great Red Dragon called the Devill and Satan, who also gave his power to the Beast, they overcame him I say) by the Blood of that Lamb, and by that word of their Testimony, and they loved not their lives unto the death.

Now touching *Iohn Crandall* aforesaid, to whose charge they had also nothing to lay, but his being with us, owning the same Faith, and Order of the Gospell, and therefore refusing to stoop to that likenesse thereto, which they had set up; yet as is said, they sentenced him to pay 5 pounds by the next Court of Assistants, or else to be well whipt. Whereupon the day following he inquired of the Keeper, when that Court of Assistants would be, (being resolved not to chuse his punishment, they being not able to make it appear by the Law of God or Man that he was a Transgressor so to be punished) and being by him informed that it would be a quarrer of a yeer before that time came; and also, that if he were so resolved, he might put in Bail for his appearance at the time aforesaid, and so depart, he forthwith put in Bail, and so departed to visit his Family, being distant from thence threescore and ten miles. He was no sooner at home, but his Spirit was unsatisfied in what he had done, in leaving us behind in the Prison, though with our consent and counsell he did what he did; whereupon, leaving his Harvest upon the spoyl, within a few dayes he returned to us again, and tendered his person unto the Keeper, who refused it, saying, Since your departure I perceive your Sentence is, That you should not depart the Prison, without either paying the money, or putting in security for the payment of it; wherefore now either you or your Surety must pay it. To whom Brother *Crandall* replyed, you informed me otherwise before I went, and upon other termes I departed, wherefore for my own part I am resolved I will not pay it, and for my Surety he is at his liberty, being no otherwise bound, than for my appearance, and here I am, and am your Prisoner; neverthelesse when I was released, and turned out of Prison, and could no longer upon that account there remain, I counselled him to put the matter quite out of doubt, wherefore he said to the Iaylor, Let me know what I shall trust to, for if you accept me upon the former account, well, I shall willingly tarry, and remain your Prisoner, but if not, I shall now repair home with my Friend to my Family; so after the Iaylor had advised with the Magistrate, he friendly told him, If he would promise to appear at the time appointed, he would take his word, become his Surety, and he might be gone; whereupon I being doubtfull, though he was confident concerning the time (there being an other Court between) desired him to send us certain word to the Iland, when that Court of Assistants would be; so having his promise, we thankfully accepted his kindnesse, & so departed: And being at home we waited for a word from the Keeper for a return, but the first word we heard touching that matter, was, that the Court was past (which was that Court I suspected) & that Brother *Holmes* had had his tryal by cruel scourgings, & that the Iaylor being Brother *Crandals* Surety, by reason of his non-appearance was constrained to pay the money; hereupon not long after Brother *Crandall* went to *Boston*, and charged the Iaylor with his mis-information, and neglect of his promise; and moreover declared that he had told him, That being Innocent, he would not make himself a Transgressor by chusing his punishment, and therefore had resolved, as he also knew, not to pay them a penny; and further he told him, that there was no necessity he should lay down the money, it being but through a mistake, and he being but Surety, when the Principall was present; and was able through the strength of Christ to answer the penalty: and thus having argued the case with the Iaylor, he left him without any grounds of hope to have it repaid, neverthelesse if advantage will be so strictly taken upon the Keepers mistake, neither Conscience nor Equity will suffer us (it appearing to be a meer mistake, and no plotted thing) not to suffer him to bear it, and thus it appears how a second came off, and escaped a scourging: Now as concerning the third, by name *Obe-*

diah Holmes, what is laid to his charge this Sentence
under their Secretaries hand (a Copy whereof is here
under written) will plainly expresse.

The Sentence of Obediah Holmes *of* Seacuck, *the* 31 *of
the 5th M.* 1651.

Forasmuch as you *Obediah Holmes*, being come into
this Iurisdiction about the 21 *of the 5th M.* did meet at
one *William Witters* house at *Lin*, and did hear privately
(and at other times being an Excommunicate person did
take upon you to Preach and to Baptize) upon the Lords
day, or other dayes, and being taken then by the Constable, and coming afterward to the Assembly at *Lin*, did in
disrespect of the Ordinance of God and his Worship, keep
on your hat, the Pastor being in Prayer, insomuch that
you would not give reverence in veiling your hat, till it
was forced off your head to the disturbance of the Congregation, and professing against the Institution of the
Church, as not being according to the Gospell of Iesus
Christ, and that you the said *Obediah Holmes* did upon
the day following meet again at the said *William Witters*,
in contempt to Authority, you being then in the custody
of the Law, and did there receive the Sacrament, being
Excommunicate, and you did Baptize such as were Baptized before, and thereby did necessarily deny the Baptism
that was before administred to be Baptism, the Churches
no Churches, and also other Ordinances, and Ministers,
as if all were a Nullity; And also did deny the lawfullness of Baptizing of Infants, and all this tends to the
dishonour of God, the despising the ordinances of God
among us, the peace of the Churches, and seducing the
Subjects of this Commonwealth from the truth of the
Gospel of Iesus Christ, and perverting the strait waies of
the Lord, the Court doth fine you 30 pounds to be paid,
or sufficient sureties that the said sum shall be paid by
the first day of the next Court of Assistants, or else to be
well whipt, and that you shall remain in Prison till it be
paid, or security given in for it.

By the Court,   ENCREASE NOWELL.

And now because his sufferings, and the scence which

his Soul felt of the Lords Support, according to promise, is affectionately set forth, and commended as a token of his love, in a Letter written with his own hand, and sent unto those that have obtained like precious faith in *London*, or elsewhere, whereby by an experiment which God hath been pleased to give to him, and us, they may evidently discern, that Iesus Christ is in point of tender compassions touching those that confess his name before the Sonnes of men, the same to day that he was yesterday; that as yesterday, so to day it may be said, as the sufferings of Christ abound in us, so our consolation also aboundeth by Christ, so that they which keep the commandements of God, and Testimony of Iesus Christ, may be hereby incouraged to fear none of those things which they shall suffer before they come, nor when they look them in the face, and begin the incounter with them, be soon weary and wax faint in their minds, but faithfully and hopefully expect (they suffering for the name of Christ, and as Christians) that the spirit of their Lord, and of glory, shall rest upon them. The words of his Letter followeth.

Unto the well beloved Brethren Iohn Spilsbury, William Kiffin, *and the rest that in London stand fast in that Faith, and continue to walk stedfastly in that Order of the Gospell which was once delivered unto the Saints by Iesus Christ.* Obediah Holmes *an unworthy witness, that Iesus is the Lord, and of late a Prisoner for Iesus sake at* Boston, *sendeth greeting.*

Dearly Beloved and longed after,
My hearts desire is to hear from you, and to hear that you grow in grace, and in the knowledge of our Lord and Saviour Iesus Christ, and that your love to him, and one unto another, as he hath given commandment, aboundeth, would be the very joy and great rejoycing of my Soul and Spirit; had I not been prevented by my beloved Brethren of *Providence*, who have wrot unto you, (wherein you have my Mind at large) and also by our beloved Brother *Clarke* of *Road*-Iland, who may (if God permit) see you, and speak with you mouth to mouth, I had here declared my self in that matter, but now I forbear; And

because I have an experimentall knowledge in my self, that in members of the same Body, while it stands in union with the head, there is a sympathizing Spirit, which passeth through, and also remain in each particular, so that one member can neither mourn nor rejoyce, but all the members are ready to mourn or rejoyce with it ; I shall the rather impart unto you some dealings which I have had therein from the Sons of Men, and the gracious supports which I have met with from the Son of God, my Lord, and yours, that so like Members you might rejoyce with me, and might be encouraged by the same experiment of his tender mercies, to fear none of those things which you shall suffer for Iesus sake.   It pleased the Father of Light, after a long continuance of mine in death, and darknesse, to cause life and immortality to be brought to light in my soul, and also to cause me to see that this life was by the death of his Son, in that hour, and power of darknesse procured, which wrought in my heart a restless desire to know what that Lord, who had so dearly bought me, would have me to do, and finding that it was his last will (to which none is to adde, and from which none is to detract) that they which had faith in his death for life, should yeeld up themselves to hold forth a lively consimilitude, or likenesse unto his death, buriall, and resurrection by that Ordinance of Baptisme ; I readily yeelded thereto being by love constrained to follow that Lamb (that takes away the sins of the World) whither soever he goes ; I had no sooner separated from their assemblies, and from Communion with them in their worship of God and thus visibly put on Christ, being resolved alone to attend upon him, and to submit to his will, but immediately the adversary cast out a flood against us, and stirred up the spirits of men to present my self and two more to *Plymouth* Court, where we met with 4 Petitions against our whole company to take some speedy course to suppress us, one from our own Plantation with 35 hands to it, one fro the Church (as they call it) at *Tanton*, one from all the Ministers in our Colony, except two, if I mistake not, and one from the Court at *Boston* in the *Mathatusets* under their Secretaries hand ; whereupon the Court straitly chargeth us to desist, and neither

to ordain Officers, nor to Baptize, nor to break bread together, nor yet to meet upon the first day of the week,
and having received these strait charges one of the three
discovers the sandy foundation upon which he, stood, who
when the flood came, and the wind blew, fell, yet it pleased
the Father of mercies (to whom be the praise) to give us
strength to stand, & to tell them it was better to obey
God, rather than man, and such was the grace of our God
to us-ward that though we were had from Court to Court,
yet were we firmly resolved to keep close to the rule and
to obey the voyce of our Lord, come what will come;
Not long after these troubles I came upon occasion of
businesse into the Colony of the *Mathatusets*, with two
other Brethren, as Brother *Clark*, being one of the two,
can inform you, where we three were apprehended, carried
to the prison at *Boston*, and so to the Court, and were all
sentenced; what they laid to my charge, you may here
read in my sentence : Vpon the pronouncing of which as
I went from the Bar, I exprest my self in these words;
I blesse God I am counted worthy to suffer for the name
of Iesus; whereupon *Iohn Wilson* (their Pastor as they
call him) strook me before the Iudgment Seat, and cursed
me, saying, The Curse of God, or Iesus goe with thee;
so we were carried to the Prison, where not long after I
was deprived of my two loving Friends; at whose departure the Adversary stept in, took hold on my Spirit, and
troubled me for the space of an hour, and then the Lord
came in, and sweetly releeved me, causing me to look to
himself, so was I stayed, and refreshed in the thoughts of
my God; and although during the time of my Imprisonment, the Tempter was busie, yet it pleased God so to
stand at my right hand, that the motions were but sudden,
and so vanished away; and although there were that
would have payd the money if I would accept it, yet I
durst not accept of deliverance in such a way, and therefore my answer to them was, that although I would acknowledge their love to a cup of cold·Water, yet could
I not thank them for their money if they should pay it;
so the Court drew neer, and the night before I should
suffer according to my sentence, it pleased God I rested,
and slept quietly; in the morning many Friends came to

visit me, desiring me to take the refreshment of Wine, and other Comforts, but my resolution was not to drink Wine, nor strong drink that day untill my punishment were over, and the reason was, lest in case I had more strength, courage, and boldnesse than ordinarily could be expected, the VVorld should either say he is drunk with new VVine, or else that the comfort and strength of the Creature hath carried him through, but my course was this: I desired Brother *John Hazell* to bear my Friends company, and I betook myself to my Chamber, where I might communicate with my God, commit my self to him, and beg strength from him; I had no sooner sequestred my self, and come into my Chamber, but *Sathan* lets flie at me, saying, Remember thy self, thy birth, breeding, and friends, thy wife, children, name, and credit but as this was sudden, so there came in sweetly from the Lord as sudden an answer, 'tis for my Lord, I must not deny him before the Sons of men (for that is to set men above him) but rather lose all, yea wife, children, and mine own life also: To this the tempter replies, Oh! but that is the question, is it for him? and for him alone? is it not rather for thy own, or some others sake? thou hast so professed and practised, and now art loth to deny it; is not pride and self in the bottom? surely this temptation was strong, and thereupon I made diligent search after the matter, as formerly I had done, and after a while there was even as it had been a voyce from Heaven in my very Soul, bearing witnes with my Conscience, that it was not for any mans case or sake in this world, that so I had professed and practised, but for my Lords case, and sake, and for him alone, whereupon my spirit was much refresht; as also in the consideration of these three Scriptures, which speak on this wise, *Who shall lay any thing to the charge of Gods elect? Although I walk through the valley and shadow of Death I will fear none evill, thy rod and thy staff they shall comfort me. And he that continueth to the end, the same shall be saved.* But then came in the consideration of the weaknesse of the Flesh to bear the strokes of a whip, though the Spirit was willing, and hereupon I was caused to pray earnestly unto the Lord, that he would be pleased to give me a spirit of courage and boldnesse, a tongue to speak for him, and strength of body to suffer for his sake, and not to shrink or yeeld to the stroaks, or shed tears, lest the adversaries of the truth should thereupon blaspheme, and be hardned, and the weak and feeble-hearted discouraged, and for this I besought the Lord earnestly, at length he satisfied my spirit, to give up as my soul, so my body to him, and quietly to leave the whole disposing of the matter to him, and so I addressed my self in as comely a manner as I could, having such a Lord and Master to serve in this businesse: And when I heard the voyce of my Keeper come for me, even cheerfulnesse did come upon me, and taking my Testament in my hand, I went along with him to the place of execution, and after common salutation there stood; there stood by also one of the Magistrates, by name Mr. *Encrease Nowell*, who for a while kept silent, and spoke not a word, and so did I, expecting the Governours presence, but he came not. But after a while Mr. *Nowell* bad the Executioner doe his Office, then I desired to speak a few words, but Mr. *Nowell* answered, it is not now a time to speak, whereupon I took leave, and said, Men, Brethren, Fathers, and Countrey-men, I beseech you give me leave to speak a few words, and the rather, because here are many Spectators to see me punished, and I am to seal with my Blood, if God give strength, that which I hold and practise in reference to the Word of God, and the testimony of Iesus; that which I have to say in brief is this, Although I confesse I am no Disputant, yet seeing I am to seal what I hold with my Blood, I am ready to defend it by the Word, and to dispute that point with any that shall come forth to withstand it. Mr. *Nowell* answered me, now was no time to dispute, then said I, then I desire to give an account of the Faith and Order I hold, and this I desired three times, but in comes Mr. *Flint*, and saith to the Executioner, Fellow, doe thine Office, for this Fellow would but make a long Speech to delude the people; so I being resolved to speak, told the people; That which I am to suffer for, is for the Word of God, and testimony of Iesus Christ; No, saith Mr. *Nowell* it is for your Error, and going about to seduce the people; to which I replyed, not for Error, for in all the time of my Imprisonment, wherein

I was left alone (my Brethren being gone) which of all your Ministers in all that time came to convince me of Error? and when upon the Governours words a motion was made for a publick dispute, and upon fair terms so often renewed, and desired by hundreds, what was the reason it was not granted? Mr. *Nowell* told me, it was his fault that went away, and would not dispute; but this the Writings will cleer at large: still Mr. *Flint* calls to the man to doe his Office, so before, and in the time of his pulling off my cloathes I continued speaking, telling them, That I had so learned, that for all *Boston* I would not give my bodie into their hands thus to be bruised upon another account, yet upon this I would not give the hundredth part of a * *Wampon Peague* to free it out of their hands, and that I made as much Conscience of unbuttoning one button, as I did of paying the 30l. in reference thereunto; I told them moreover, the Lord having manifested his love towards me, in giving me repentance towards God, and Faith in Iesus Christ, and so to be baptized in water by a Messenger of Iesus into the name of the Father, Son, and Holy Spirit, wherein I have fellowship with him in his death, buriall, and resurrection, I am now come to be baptized in afflictions by your hands, that so I may have further fellowship with my Lord, and am not ashamed of his sufferings, for by his stripes am I healed; And as the man began to lay the stroaks upon my back, I said to the people, though my Flesh should fail, and my Spirit should fail, yet God would not fail; so it pleased the Lord to come in, and so to fill my heart and tongue as a vessell full, and with an audible voyce I brake forth, praying unto the Lord not to lay this Sin to their charge, and telling the people, That now I found he did not fail me, and therefore now I should trust him for ever who failed me not; for in truth, as the stroaks fell upon me, I had such a spirituall manifestation of Gods presence, as the like thereunto I never had, nor felt, nor can with fleshly tongue expresse, and the outward pain was so removed from me, that indeed I am not able to declare it to you, it was so easie to me, that I could well

---

* A *Wampon Peague* is the sixth part of a penny with us.

bear it, yea and in a manner felt it not, although it was
grievous, as the Spectators said, the Man striking with all
his strength (yea spitting on his hand three times, as
many affirmed) with a three-coarded whip, giving me
therewith thirty stroaks; when he had loosed me from
the Post, having joyfulnesse in my heart, and cheerfulnesse in my countenance, as the Spectators observed, I
told the Magistrates, you have struck me as with Roses;
and said moreover, Although the Lord hath made it easie
to me, yet I pray God it may not be laid to your charge.
After this many came to me, rejoycing to see the power of
the Lord manifested in weak flesh; but sinfull flesh takes
occasion hereby to bring others in trouble, informs the
Magistrates hereof, and so two more are apprehended as
for contempt of authority, there names were *Iohn Hazell*
and *Iohn Spur*, who came indeed and did shake me by the
hand, but did use no words of contempt or reproach unto
any; no man can prove that the first spoke any thing,
and for the second, he only said thus, Blessed be the
Lord; yet these two for taking me by the hand, and thus
saying after I had received my punishment, were sentenced to pay 40 shillings, or to be whipt. Both were resolved against paying their Fine: Neverthelesse after one
or two dayes imprisonment, one payed *Iohn Spurs* Fine,
and he was released, and after six or seven dayes Impris
onment of Brother *Hazell*, even the day when he should
have suffered, an other payd his, and so he escaped, and
the next day went to visit a Friend about 6 miles from
Boston, where he the same day fell sick, and within 10
dayes he ended this life; when I was come to the Prison,
it pleased God to stir up the heart of an old acquaintance
of mine, who with much tendernesse, like the good *Samaritan*, poured oyl into my wound, and plaistered my sores;
but there was present information given what was done,
and inquiry made who was the Chirurgion, and it was
commonly reported he should be sent for, but what was
done, I yet know not. Now thus it hath pleased the
Father of Mercies so to dispose of the matter, that my
Bonds and Imprisonments have been no hinderance to
the Gospel, for before my return, some submitted to the
Lord, and were baptized, and divers were put upon the

way of enquiry; And now being advised to make my
escape by night, because it was reported that there were
Warrants forth for me, I departed; and the next day
after, while I was on my Iourney, the Constable came to
search at the house where I lodged, so I escaped their
hands, and was by the good hand of my heavenly Father
brought home again to my neer relations, my wife, and
eight children, the Brethren of our Town, and *Providence*
having taken pains to meet me 4 miles in the woods,
where we rejoyced together in the Lord. Thus have I
given you as briefly as I can, a true relation of things:
wherefore my Brethren rejoyce with me in the Lord, and
give all glory to him, for he is worthy, to whom be praise
for evermore, to whom I commit you, and put up my earnest prayers for you, that by my late experience, who
have trusted in God, and have not been deceived, you may
trust in him perfectly: wherefore my dearly beloved Brethren trust in the Lord, and you shall not be ashamed, nor
confounded, so I also rest,

Yours in the bond of Charity,
Obediah Holmes.

Three things would be well minded in this relation,
1 that God gave me Power to confess his name before
the Sonnes of Men.

2 That he kept my tongue that I did not not speak
evill of men, nor of Authority.

3 That he gave strength to weak Flesh that it failed
not.

This Tragedy being thus acted in the face of the Country, must needs awaken and rouse up the minds, and
spirits of many, cause sad thoughts to arise in their
hearts, and to flow forth at their mouthes as men offended, to see Strangers professing Godliness, so discourteous-
ly used, for no Civill Transgression, but meerly for Conscience, and that by their hands who pretended, that
Liberty of Conscience was also the cause of their flight,
together with the other to the hazard of their lives by
hard hearted, cruell, and savage *Barbarians,* and other
mischiefs which a vast, and howling Wildernesse is apt
to produce; wherefore to stop their mouthes, and to lull

them asleep, the old subtile Serpent as his custome ever hath been, raised up a cloud of disgrace, thinking thereby to darken the truth he profest, and to obscure the glory that appeared in his sufferings, giving out, that he was but an Excommunicate, and so an accursed person, and that it was vehemently suspected, that he was notoriously given to that filthy lust of uncleanness, which God will judge, and that the same was hinted in open Court, and that by persons of no mean credit; wherefore againe to resist the adversary who hath been a lyer from the beginning, and thereby a destroyer and murderer, and to deliver the Children of truth at least from his snare, whereby they might be taken captive at his will, he drew up, and sent a letter unto the Governour of the *Mathatusetts* Colony, and desired it might be published so that the Sons of Men, so far as the lye and slander might spread, might be acquainted therewith. The Letter followeth.

The 12 *of the* 7*th. M.* 51. *To the Honoured Governour.*

Honoured Sir,

However you may judge of me, yet am I dayly waiting to stand before him who shall judge quick and dead, and now because I am under reproach, and sensure by many, and the more by reason of some words spoken by yourself, as though I were an evill person in life and conversation, and although I may be accounted as a fool, yet hear me a little to plead mine innocency, and I hope you will not too far condemn me untill you hear me speak; Sir, I acknowledge only free grace, and that by his power alone I have been kept, and what my life and manner of conversation was for six. or seven years while I was with you, I appeal to your self, and the experiences you have had of me, and to your Elders, and to the whole Church; who ever reproved me of evill? and ye recommended me to others, and for four years time I walked with them at *Rehoboth*, who also should have reproved me if under Sin; but when it pleased the Lord to cause me to hear his voice, and I separated from them, which was occasioned by an unrighteous Act of theirs as I judged, which was, that seven of the Brethren should pass an Act of Admonition **upon a Brother without the Consent of the rest, we being**

23 in number, who might all in one hours space, if in
health, have come together, so when I heard of it I went
to Mr. *Newman*, and told him of the evill which he, and
the other six had done, he told me they were the Church
Representative, and if 4 of them had done it, it had been
a Church Act; when this comes to the Congregation, with
much adoe, he got five more to himself, and then they
were 12, and we eleven, then they owned themselves to
be the Church, and so began to deal with me for saying,
they had abused the Church, and had took from them
their power, whereupon I told them I should renounce
them, and not have any more fellowship with them, till
either they saw their Sin, or I further light; after which
divers others to the number of seven, or eight fell off from
them, and we met once a week, and every first day, and
so continued for a long space of time, yea and the day was
known when we intended to be Baptized, and there were
many Witnesses observing our Faith, and Order, and yet
not one Man or Woman of Mr. *Newmans* company that
ever came to deal with me for evill, neither in Judgment,
nor Practice, untill a long time after that appointment of
our Lord was dispensed; Thus I say, when I had separated from them, and a long time after, I understood by their
Messenger that they intended to proceed against me, so I
desired the messenger to tell me for what evill, he told
me I should know when I come there, so I sent one of
their own Brethren to tell them from me, though I owned
them not as Brethren, yet if any Man or Woman had
ought against me, I would come to them, although they
had not delt with me according to any rule; but none
came to me, nor charged me with any evill; and when upon
occasion I came before all the Congregation, and strangers,
I demanded for what cause it was that they proceeded
against me, seeing I had sent to them before, and no man
accused me; Mr. *Newman* told me, it was for nonappear-
ance; and now judge of the evill in your own way, and
that for my Excommunication as you call it, I am by you
rendred that wicked person; as for the suspition of that
most abominable evill of uncleanness, and Adultery, which
many think I am guilty of, by reason of some persons
speeches, I desire to bless my Lord, who hath caused me
to deny all uncleanness and wickedness, and God forbid

that I should take the Members of Christ, and make them
the Members of an Harlot, and I challenge all Men and
Women that dare stand before the judgment seat of the
Lord, to come forth, and say if they ever heard unclean
words proceed out of my mouth, or any unseemly gesture,
much less action, to any in my life at *Salem, Seacunk,* or
elswhere, yea let them come forth before any to meet me
in private, or publick, upon any friends request without
the Magistrates Warrant; but I remember my Lord was
called Belzebub, and what though I be called an Adul-
terer, or Witch, or Blasphemer, and every one saith what
he pleaseth, yet I stand before the judgment of my Lord;
And whereas it was also reported I Baptized Goodwife
Bowdish naked, I bless the Lord he hath taught me to do
that which is comly, and of good report, yea and I know
a Man, or Woman may be drowned in their Cloathes, or
buryed in earth with their Cloathes, but that she had
comly garments from the Crown of her head to the sole
of her foot, many being present with her husband can testifie and if any be pleased to reproach me behind my back,
and not to speak to my face, let them know the Lord
knows how to deliver the innocent, unto whom I commit
myself, with my prayers for you, and am,

Yours still as formerly to command in all
Lawfull things
Obediah Holmes.

Whilst (he through the spirit of the Lord that rested
upon him) bore these bloody strokes with so cheerfull a
spirit as if he felt them not, divers of the standers by, beholding it, were so affected with joy, that when he was
loosed could not forbear to come to him, and to shake
him by the hand, thereby to manifest their rejoycing with
him, that the Lord had supported him; but information
hereof being given to the Magistrates, warrants were sent
forth (as is reported to the number of 13) whereupon
some through fear were fain to hide themselves, and being
strangers, to hasten away, or change their habit, two of
them were taken as aforesaid, that is to say *John Spur,*
and old *Iohn Hazell,* and committed to prison as the Warrant herewith declares.

To the Keeper or his Deputy.

By virtue hereof you are to take into your custody, and safe keeping, the body of Iohn Spur *for a hainous offence by him committed, hereof not to fail. Dated the 5th. of the 7th. Month* 1651. *Take also into your safe keeping* Iohn Hazell. By the Court,

INCREASE NOWEL.

Iohn Spur profest to me, and before many Witnesses, that his heart was so taken with what he saw and heard, that he could not but go to him, take him by the hand, and blesse the Lord who had been so present with him, but to save me a labor his own words here followeth.

Mr. *Cotton* (saith he) in his Sermon immediately before the Court gave their Sentence against M. *Clark, Obediah Holmes*, and *Iohn Crandall*, affirmed, that denying Infants Baptism would overthrow all; and this was a capitall offence; and therefore they were foul-murtherers; when therefore the Governor M. *Iohn Indicot* came into the Court to pass Sentence against them, he said thus, you deserve to dy, but this we agreed upon, that Mr. *Clarke* shall pay 20 li. Fine, and *Obediah Holmes* 30 li. Fine, and *Jo. Crandall* 5 li. Fine, and to remain in prison untill their Fines be either payed or security given for them, or else they are all of them to be well whipped; When *Obediah Holmes* was brought forth to receive his Sentence, he desired of the Magistrates, that he might hold forth the ground of his practice; but they refused to let him speak, and commanded the whipper to do his Office; then the whipper began to pull off his Cloathes, upon which *Obediah Holmes* said, Lord lay not this sin unto their charge; and so the whipper began to lay on with his whip; upon which *Obediah Holmes* said, O Lord I beseech thee to manifest thy power in the weaknesse of thy Creature; he neither moving nor stirring at all for the strokes, brake out into these expressions, Blessed and praised be the Lord, and thus he carryed it to the end, and went away rejoycingly; I *Iohn Spur* being present, it did take such an impression in my Spirit to trust in God, and to walk according to the light that God had communicated to me, and not to fear what man could do unto me; that I went to the man (being inwardly affected with what I saw and heard) and with a joyfull countenance took him by the hand when he was from the Post, and said, praised be the Lord; and so I went along with him to the prison; and presently that day there was information given to the Court what I had said and done; and also a warrant was presently granted out that day to arest both myself and *Iohn Hazel*, which was executed on the morrow morning upon us, and so we were brought to the Court and examined; the Governour asked me concerning *Obediah Holmes*, according as he was informed by old Mr. *Cole* and *Thomas Buttolph*, of my taking of him by the hand, and smiling, and I did then freely declare what I did, and what I said, which was this; *Obediah Holmes*, said I, I do look upon as a Godly man; and do affirm that he carryed himself as did become a Christian, under so sad an affliction; and his affliction did so affect my Soul, that I went to him being from the Post, and said, blessed be the Lord, but said the Governour what do you apprehend concerning the cause for which he suffered? my Answer was, that I am not able to judge of it, then said the Governour, we will deal with you as we have dealt with him, I said unto him again, I am in the hands of God, then Mr. *Simons* a Magistrate said, you shall know you are in the hands of Men; the Governour then said, keeper take him, and so I was presently carried away to prison.

The next day about one of the Clock I was sent for again into the Court; the Governour (being then about to go out of the Court, when I came in) delivered this speech to me; said he, you must pay 40 shillings or be whipped; I said then to those of the Court that remained, that if any man suffer as a Christian let him glorifie God in this behalf, then I desired to know what Law I had broken, and what evill I had done, but they produced no Law, only they produced what the two witnesses had sworn against me; my speech thereto was this, my practice and cariage is alowed by the word of God, for it is written in *Rom.* 12. *Be like affectioned one towards another, rejoyce with them that rejoyce;* and it is contrary to my ludgment and Conscience to pay a peny; then said Mr. *Bendall*, I will pay it for him, and there presented himself;

I answered then and said, I thanked him for his love, but did believe it was no acceptable service, for any man to pay a peny for me in this case; yet notwithstanding the Court accepted of his profer, and bid me be gone, then came *Iohn Hazell* to be examined.

Iohn Spur.

Here followeth the testimony of those that came in against me.

I · *Cole* being in the Market place, when *Obediah Holmes* came from the Whipping Post, *Iohn Spur* came and met him presently, laughing in his face, saying, Blessed be God for thee Brother, and so did go with him, laughing upon him up towards the prison, which was very grievous to me to see him harden the man in his sin, and shewing much contempt of Authority by that cariage, as if he had been unjustly punished, and had suffered as a righteous man, under a tyranicall Government. Deposed before the Court the 5th. of the 7th. M. 1651.

Increase Nowell.

I Thomas Buttolph did see *John Spur* come to *Obediah Holmes*, so soon as he came from the Whipping Post, laughing in his face, and going along with him towards the Prison to my great grief to see him harden him in his sin, and to shew such a contempt of Authority. Deposed the 5th. of the 7th. Month 1651. Before the Court.

Increase Nowell.

As for *Iohn Hazell*, to my knowledge, although he had some occasion of business in these parts, yet the main business that drew him hither, was to visit the prisoner, whom he at this time took by the hand, who was indeed his neer Neighbour, lived in the same Town together, walked together in the same fellowship, and faith of the Gospell, and had their hearts knit together in a more than ordinary neer bond of love, and as a manifestation thereof, he undertoke so great a journey (it being between fourty and fifty miles) to visit him, he being indisposed by reason of his age for such an undertaking (being between three and fourscore years old) and when he was there understanding it would not be long before he should suffer, out of the same tender love, could not leave him before it was over; who also accompanied him from the Prison to the Post, and so back again; now for him, only for taking his friend by the hand, when he had suffered his punishment, and was loosed from the Post, to be thus handled, shall not the Nations that know not civility, that neither fear God nor reverence man, be astonished at this? if this be to do to others as we would that others should do to us, which is the Law and the Prophets, the command of Christ and his Apostles, let all true Christians judge; the Man being old did professe, as I was informed, That if they should have laid the strokes upon him, they would certainly have killed him, which I know ceized not a little upon him, and how far what was done had influence into his death, the Lord onely knowes; for as is before said, the same day he went forth, he fell sick, and within ten dayes he died; The Lord grant that no part of his death may be laid to their charge, and that they may see the exceeding greatnesse of the evill of thirsting after the blood of the Innocent, before the Lord come forth to avenge it, and as to that story I shall say no more, but leave the Reader to his own relation, which partly in Prison, and partly upon his death Bed, as may be perceived, he wrote and left behind him, with an intent it should be published. The relation followeth, writ and subscribed with his own hand.

A Relation of my being brought before the Magistrates the 6th of the 7th Moneth, 1651.

I Going from place to place, to buy and take up commodities for my use, was attached or arrested by the Marshall, by virtue of a Warrant from the Court, to appear in the Court, and there to answer for a high misdemeanor committed by me, and coming into the Court (which was then privately kept in the Chamber) they asked me divers questions, amongst which this was one; Whether I did think that *Obediah Holmes* did well or not, in comming among them to baptize, and administer the Sacrament, laying this to my charge, that I was one with him, and of the same judgement, and whether I did think he did well, or no, in his so carrying himself; to which I answered, I had here nothing to doe with that which another Man did, but I was here to answer for what I myself had committed against their Law; then said they, you have offended our Law, and have contemned Authority, for you took him by the hand, and did countenance him in his sin, so soon as he was gone from the Post, to which I said, If I have broken any Law of the place, by what I then did, I am willing to submit unto punishment; yea said the Governour, you took him by the hand, did you not? and spake to him, what said you? did you not say so and so? Blessed be God, &c. To which I said, I shall refer myself unto the testimonies that may or can be brought against me; well, said the Governour, wee shall find Testimony enough against you; take him to you Keeper, and we will call you forth in publick for that we doe with you we will proceed in publick with you, and so I went to Prison. This was the sum and substance of the first time I was called before them; the next day being the last day of the week, and the last day of their Court, I was in expectation all the forenoon to be called forth, but was not, so after dinner, when (as it appeareth) the Court was risen, and some of the Magistrates departed, I was sent for again into the Chamber, where was the Governor with three others, *scil.* Mr. *Bellingham,* Mr. *Hibbins,* and Mr. *Encrease Nowell,* as soon as I was come into the room, the Governour read my Sentence, which was, that I must pay 40 sh. or be well whipt, and so immediately he departed, and when he was gone (for I could not have time before) I answered, that I desired the privilege of an English Subject, which was to be tryed by the Country, to wit, a Jury, and to be made to appear (if they can) to be a Transgressor by a Law: To which they said, I had contemned Authority, and they had a Law to punish such, and said they, you did shew your contempt of Authority, in that you did take such a person by the hand, as soon as he was from the Post. To which I answered, I could not doe that which I did in contempt to Authority, seeing he had satisfied the Law to the full, and was departed from the place of suffering; and in the next place what I did, I did unto him as my Friend; And further I said, if I had taken him by the hand so soon as he was loosed from the Post, and had led him out of the Town, I should not have broken any Law either of God or Man. To this they said, That there was a Law in all Courts of Justice, both in Old *England*, and other Countreyes, to punish contempt of Authority, and so had they such a Law among themselves; To which I said, That in Old *England*, and in other places they had such a Law I denyed not, but that Law also was both Enacted and published, but what Law have I broken in taking my Friend by the hand, when he was free, and had satisfied the Law? To this they replied, That he had not satisfied the Keeper; To this I answered, That he had talked with his Keeper, and there was some Agreement between them, and so in that sence also not under the Law, but free; Then said they, if you would have shewed kindnesse unto your Friend, you might have forborn in that place, and done it more privately; To which I answered, I knew not but that place was as free as another, he having satisfied the Law. The Testimony that was given by Mr. *Cole* was this, *sci. I saw* Iohn Hazell *take* Obediah Holmes *by the hand, but what he said I cannot tell;* this is the Substance of all the proceedings untill the last day at night, and then they said I should be whipped, but said some of their Officers, the Whipper cannot be found, then they commanded that they should be ready by the second day morning, and then I did expect to be called forth, but neither that day, nor the third, nor fourth, was I called, but am as I understand reserved unto the 5th day, to be more publick in the view of the World, and when the 5th day came, as I had many before, so also then, that would have paid the Fine, if I would give my consent, which I denyed to doe, and so set myself by the power of Christ to suffer what should be inflicted upon me, but when Noon came I was told I should not suffer whipping, yet not having a discharge, I did not look to be freed untill the Keeper told me, I might goe about my businesse; then I demanded a discharge (meaning under the Magistrates hands) so he bad me goe, he would discharge me.

The strokes I was enjoyned by the Court to have, were 10 with a three-corded whip, the very same number I understand, that the worst Malefactors that were there punished had, of which some were guilty of common Whoredom, other of forcing a little Child, and one *Indian* for coyning of money; thus far have you a relation according to my best remembrance from the first to the last, of all the passages concerning this matter; By me *Iohn Hazell*, written with mine own hand in *Boston* Prison, the 13 day of the 7th moneth, 1651.

A Postscript. Since I wrot, I understand there is a report that I was willing to pay my Fine, and that the Magistrates would not accept of it without I were willing. Gentle Reader, be pleased to understand that this is false, for it was without my consent or approbation; and further understand, That the Fine was taken by them, upon the profer of Mr. *Bendall* for *Iohn Spur*, it was willingly accepted by the Magistrates, and approved of, although *Iohn Spur* did to their faces contradict it, and oppose it; therefore good Reader beleeve not such reports.

By me *Iohn Hazell.*

Now of what hath been spoken in this Narrative (Reader) this is the sum.

1. Thou maist understand that the next morning after we three, being strangers, were come to our friends house at Lin where we lodged, (it being two miles out of the town) we were persued and also apprehended by the Constables under the name of erronious persons being strangers, and by that power were caried (after a full and clear manifestation of our unfreeness) unto their Assembly, then to Prison, and after a while were also brought before their Iudgment seat; in which two Assemblies, to which we were forced, they drew forth matter enough as they conceived to make us transgressors, and thereupon proceeded to sentence us without producing either Accuser, Witness, Iury, Law of God, or man, whereby either we might appear to be guilty, or they to be just and justified in their proceedings against us.

2. After we were thus persued, and apprehended under the name of erronious persons and strangers, and by their Court condemned and sentenced as Herericks or scismaticks, a motion being made by their Governour touching a discourse with their Ministers, was readily accepted by us,

and often repeated, and as often promised by them, but yet could not be obtained, as is here at large to be seen.

3. Although through the mercifull hand of our God upon us, we had wronged no man, corrupted no man, defrauded no man, as he, together with our Consciences, then did, and still to this day, do bear us witnesse yet besides the exceeding great loss and detriment otherwise sustained, we had all no doubt met with as cruell Scourgings as his faithfull servants of old, had not the provident hand of our God so disposed the hearts of some of our friends to lay down our ransome, by which two did escape; and this did evidently appear in the third who came under their zealous, yet merciless hands, and received from them 50 stripes above the restraint of the Iews, as writers report, yea and such entertainment no doubt should strangers or Angels from Heaven, yea Christ Iesus himself have received at their hands, if they could effect it, in case they should have come among them, and not submitted, (as it is not possible they should) unto that golden, and glorious Image or likeness of the worship and way of God appointed by Christ which they have set up.

4. When this faithfull Martyr and Witness, that Christ is the Lord, had born this fourscore and ten stripes cruelly laid on, not only with a patient mind, but with an exceeding great joy of the holy spirit, as the spectators could not but discern, and was loosed from the Post, and was going to Prison again, some being inwardly moved with joy in beholding the gracious support which the Lord afforded him, (as they have affirmed) could not forbear to take him by the hand, for which thing sake two of them were apprehended and sentenced to pay each of them 40s or els be whipt. Let the Actors themselves, and all that peruse their practice for cautions sake consider, whether the spirit by which they are led thus to act, be not very like unto, if not the same which is seen, Revel. 13. *Acting the second Beast that arose up out of the Earth which had two hornes like a Lamb, yet spake like a Dragon, and exercised all the power of the first Beast that was before him, caused a lively Image to be made unto him, and forced the Earth and them that dwel therein, both small and great, rich and poor, free and bond, to worship his Image, and that no*

man might buy, or sell, save he, that had the marke, or the name, or the number of his name.   Here is Wisdom! and let such as desire from their hearts to live Godly in Christ Iesus, and do as really expect to suffer with Christ in this present evill World, as they do to reign with him in that good World which is yet to come, let such I say consider, and bear still in mind these expressions, Revel. 13. 10. *He that leadeth into Captivity shall go into Captivity, he that killeth with the Sword must be killed with the Sword; here is the patience and faith of the Saints.*   Rev. 12. 11. *And they overcame him by the bloud of the Lamb, and by the Word of their Testimony, and they loved not their lives unto the death.*

Rev. 6. 9, 10, 11. *I saw under the Altar the Souls of them that were slain for the Word of God, and for the testimony which they held; And they cryed with a loud voice saying, how long holy and true wilt thou not judge and avenge our blood on them that dwel on the Earth, &c.*

Rev. 20. 4. *And I saw the Souls of them that were beheaded for the Witness of Iesus, and for the Word of God, and which had not worshiped the Beast, neither his Image, neither had received the marke upon their foreheads, or in their hands, and they lived and reigned with Christ a thousand years.*

And now forasmuch as it was boldly affirmed by a Solicitor for *New-England*, and that in the Councell Chamber before that honourable Committee there assembled in Councell, that men in *New-England* might freely injoy their understandings, and Consciences, provided they walk civilly among them, and that they that suffered of late, did not suffer for their Consciences but for some misdemeanor, thereby endeavouring to possess those noble brests with that which is false; therefore I think it necessary (both for the Vindication of truth, and to the end that such worthy persons may not be taken with, or deceived by such unworthy reports, so as to be drawn to countenance persons that walk in a way that they are ashamed in plain and open terms to profess, and acknowledge, for these ends I say I think it necessary to produce their **Laws**, at least such as speak to the matter in question, whereby these two things will plainly appear.

1. That they that will not, or else in Conscience towards God cannot conform to their worship, or suspend the worship of God as their Souls are perswaded, are by the authority of their Laws to be forced to the one, and restrained from the other, and that the Magistrate is thereby not only justified in, but also injoyned unto, such a proceeding against them, although the men otherwise walk not only as civilly or soberly as themselves, but also righteously, and Godly in this present evill World, and are such indeed as are a Law to themselves.

2. Although they have Laws thus to proceed to force all to their worship, & to restrain those that differ from them, from that worship to which their Souls are perswaded, yet in our case they were so far transported with zeal, that, what they did unto us, they did without Law, yea against those Cautions which their own Laws have provided.

Certain Lawes established in the Colony of the Mathatusets *in* New-England, *and drawn forth (by constraint) to prove that the Authority there established cannot permit men, though of never so civill, sober, and peaceable a Spirit and Life, freely to enjoy their understandings and consciences, nor yet to live, or come among them, unlesse they can doe as they doe, and say as they say, or else say nothing, and so may a man live at* Rome *also.*

It is ordered by this Court, and the Authority thereof, That no mans life shall be taken away; no mans honour or good name shall be stayned; no mans person shall be arrested, restrained, banished, dismembred nor any wayes punished; no man shall be deprived of his wife or children, no mans goods or estates shall be taken away from him; nor any wayes indamaged under colour of Law or countenance of Authoritie, unlesse it be by vertue, or equity of some expresse Law of the Country warranting the same, established by a General Court and sufficiently published; or in case of the defect of a Law in any particular case, by the word of God. And in capitall cases, or in cases concerning dismembring, or banishment, according to that word to be judged by the General Court. see p. 1.

For the suppressing of Anabaptists.

It is ordered by this Court and Authority thereof, that if any person or persons within this Iurisdiction shall either openly condemn or oppose the baptizing of Infants, or goe about secretly to seduce others from the approbation or use thereof, or shall purposely depart the Congregation at the administration of that Ordinance; or shall deny the Ordinance of Magistracy, or their lawfull right or authority to make war, or punish the outward breaches of the first Table, and shall appear to the Court wilfully and obstinately to continue therein, after due means of conviction, every such person or persons shall be sentenced to Banishment. see pag. 3.

Against Blasphemy, being a capitall transgression.

It is ordered, that if any person within this Iurisdiction, whether Christian or Pagan, shall wittingly and willingly presume to BLASPHEME the holy Name of God, Father, Son, or Holy-Ghost with direct, expresse, presumptuous, or high-handed blasphemy, either by wilfull or obstinate denying the true God, or his Creation, or Government of the World; or shall curse God in like manner, or reproach the holy Religion of God, as if it were but a politick device to keep ignorant men in awe; or shall utter any other kind of Blasphemy, of the like nature and degree, they shall be put to death. *Lev.* 24. 15, 16. See p. 5.

To raise money for Publick charges in Church and Commonwealth.

It is ordered by this Court, and the Authority thereof, that every Inhabitant shal henceforth contribute to all charges both in Church and Commonwealth whereof he doth or may receive benefit: and every such Inhabitant who shal not voluntarily contribute proportionably to his ability with the Freemen of the same Town to all comon charges, both Civil and Ecclesiastical, shall be compelled thereto by assessment and distress to be levyed by the

Constable or other Officer of the Town as in other cases:
and that the lands and estates of all men (wherever they
dwell) shall be rated for all Town charges both Civil and
Ecclesiastial as aforesaid, where the lands and estates
shall lye; their persons where they dwell. See p. 9.

Lawes Ecclesiasticall.

1 All the people of God within this Iurisdiction, who
are not in a Church way, and be orthodox in judgement,
and not scandalous in life, shall have full liberty to gather
themselves into a Church estate, provided they doe it in
a Christian way, with due observation to the rules of
Christ revealed in his word. Provided also that the General Court doth not, nor will hereafter approve of any
such companies of men as shall joyn in any pretended
way of Church fellowship, unless they shall acquaint the
Magistrates and the Elders of the neighbour Churches
where they intend to joyn, and have their approbation
therein.

2 And it is further ordered, that no person being a
member of any Church which shall be gathered without
the approbation of the Magistrates and the said Churches,
shall be admitted to the Freedom of this Common-wealth.

3 Every Church hath also free liberty to exercise all
the Ordinances of God according to the rules of the Scripture.

4 Every Church hath free liberty of election and ordi-
nation of all her Officers from time to time. Provided
they be able, pious and orthodox. Now the question is
who shall judge of these words of restraint, Christian way,
rules of the Scripture, word of God, able and orthodox.

13 That if any Christian (so called) within this Iurisdiction shall contemptously behave himself toward the
Word preached, or the Messengers thereof called to dis-
pense the same in any Congregation; when he doth faithfully execute his Service and Office therein, according to
the will and word of God either by interrupting him in
his preaching, or by charging him falsely with any errour
which he hath not taught in the open face of the Church:
or like a son of *Korah* cast upon his true doctrine or himself any reproach to the dishonour of the Lord Iesus who

hath sent him, and to the disparagement of that his holy Ordinance, and making Gods wayes contemptible and ridiculous: that every such person or persons (whatsoever censure the Church may passe) shall for the first scandal be convented and reproved openly by the Magistrate at some Lecture, and bound to their good behaviour. And if a second time they break forth into the like contemptuous carriages, they shall either pay five pounds to the publick Treasurie; or stand two hours openly upon a block or stool, four foot high, on a lecture day, with a Paper fixed on his brest, written in Capitall letters [AN OPEN AND OBSTINATE CONTEMNER OF GODS HOLY ORDINANCES] that others may fear and be ashamed of breaking out into the like wickedness.

14 It is ordered and decreed by this Court and Authority thereof, That wheresoever the ministry of the word is established according to the order of the Gospell throughout this Iurisdiction, every person shall duely resort and attend thereunto respectively upon the Lords dayes, and upon such publick Fast-days, and dayes of Thanksgiving as are to be generally kept by the appointment of Authority: and if any person within this Iurisdiction shall without just and necessary cause withdraw himself from hearing the publick ministry of the word, after due means of conviction used, he shall forfeit for his absence from every such publick meeting 5 shillings. All such offences to be heard and determined by any one Magistrate or more from time to time.

15 It is ordered by this Court, That the civil Authoritie here established hath power and liberty to see the peace, ordinances and rules of Christ to be observed in every Church according to his word. As also to deal with any church-member in a way of civil justice notwithstanding any church relation, office, or interest; so it be done in a civil and not in an ecclesiastical way. Nor shall any church censure degrade or depose any man from any civil dignity, office or authority he shall have in the Common-wealth.

It is ordered, that from henceforth all lands, cattle, and other estates of any kind whatsoever, shall be iyable to be rated to all common charges whatsoever, either for the

Church, Town or Comon-wealth in the same place where the estate is from time to time. see pag. 18, 19, 20.

Heresie.

Although no humane power be Lord over the Faith and Consciences of Men, and therefore may not constrain them to beleeve or profess against their Consciences: yet because such as bring in damnable heresies, tending to the subversion of the Christian Faith, and destruction of the soules of men, ought duly to be restrained from such notorious impiety, It is therefore ordered and decreed by this Court;

That if any Christian within this Iurisdiction shall go about to subvert and destroy the Christian Faith and Religion, by broaching or maintaining any damnable heresie; as denying the immortality of the Soul, or the resurrection of the body, or any sin to be repented of in the Regenerate, or any evil done by the outward man to be accounted sin: or denying that Christ gave himself a Ransom for our sins, or shall affirm that we are not justified by his Death and Righteousnesse, but by the perfection of our own works; or shall deny the morality of the fourth comandement, or shall indeavour to seduce others to any the heresies aforementioned, every such person continuing obstinate therein; after due means of conviction, shall be sentenced to Banishment. see pag. 24.

Disturbing of Churches.

It is ordered and decreed by this Court, and the Authority thereof, That if any person whether in Church-fellowship or not, shall goe about to destroy or disturb the orders and peace of the Churches established in this Iurisdiction, by open renouncing their Church, Estate, or their Ministry, or other ordinances dispenced in them, either upon pretence that the Churches were not planted by any new Apostles, or that ordinances are for carnall Christians, or babes in Christ, and not for spirituall, or illuminated persons, or upon any other such like grounded conceit, every such person, who shall be found culpable herein, after due means of conviction, shall forfeit to the publick Treasury forty shillings for every moneth, so long as he continues in that his obstinacy.

Torture.

That no man shall be beaten with above forty stripes for one Fact at one time. Nor shall any man be punished with whipping, except he have not otherwise to answer the Law, unlesse his crime be very shamefull, & his course of life vitious & profligate. see p. 50.

The Testimony of John Clarke, Obediah Holmes, *and* John Crandall, *Prisoners at* Boston, *in* New-England, *concerning the faith and order of the Gospel of Christ Iesus the Lord, as the same was laid down in four Conclusions, and proffered to be openly and publickly defended against all gain-sayers ; when none would come forth thus to oppose it : now again by the aforesaid* John Clarke *reviewed, particularly, and strictly examined by the Word of God, and Testimony of Iesus, and thereby, (as is here at large to be seen) confirmed and justified.*

The first Conclusion.

[*I Testifie that Iesus of* Nazareth, *whom God hath raised from the dead, is made both* Lord *and* Christ] you may see this testimony clearly, and plentifully witnessed and confirmed by the Scriptures of Truth ; for First, that God raised him from the dead, appears by the testimony of 12 chosen Witnesses, *Acts* 2. 24. 32. This Jesus, say they, hath God raised up, whereof we are Witnesses ; so also *chap.* 3. 15. And being alive again he was seen of above 500 Brethren at once being faithfull Witnesses, Children that will not lie, see 1 *Cor.* 15. 6. And last of all he was seen of *Paul,* whom he sent to the Gentiles, see 1 *Cor.* 15. 8. *Acts* 22. 18. 21. And this is layd by *Paul* as the foundation of the hope of the *Israel* of God, that they shall be raised, and shall share in that glory that shall then be revealed ; yea it is that word of Truth (as *Peter* witnesseth) by which the Father of mercies doth again beget such as had sinned & faln short of the glory of God, & were without hope, unto a lively hope of the glory of God, in an inheritance, incorruptible and undefiled, that fadeth not away, and is reserved in heaven for them, see 1 *Pet.* 1. 3. 4. And in the second place, that God hath made this Iesus whom he hath raised from the dead, both Lord and Christ, see it also confirmed *Acts* the 2d, the 36. 10. 36. 2 *Cor.* 4. 5.   *Acts* 18. 5.

[*This Iesus I say is the Christ, in* English, *the Anointed One, hath a name above every name*] that he is not onely said to be a Christ and an Anointed one, which, although it be a name of eminency among men, yet may there be found many, both before the time of Reformation, and since, upon whom this worthy name of Christ, or Anointed one may be worthily called, as were those names of eminency among the *Israel* of old, as King, Priest, and Prophet, and such as being washed in the blood of the Lamb are also Anointed, and made Kings and Priests unto God, and Prophets to men compare the 2 *Cor.* 1. 21. 1 *Io.* 2. 27. with *Rev.* 5. 10. 19. 10. I say he is not onely a Christ, but that he might appear in this eminent name to have the preheminence, he is called the Christ, see *Mark* 8. 29. *Io.* 11. 27. 6. 69. 20. 31. which in *English* is the Anointed one, as will appear, 1 *Io.* 41. We have found, saith *Andrew* to *Simon*, the *Messias*, being the *Hebrew* word, which being interpreted into the *Greek* Language, is ὁ χριςός, or the Christ but rendered in *English* as in the margent, is the Anointed, and hence he is called in the 9 *Luk.* 20. the Christ of God, or in more plain *English*, the Anointed of God, suitable to this are such expressions of the spirit of God, in the Scriptures of truth, as these; Him hath God Anointed, and that with the oyl of gladnesse above his fellowes, see *Acts* 4. 27. 10. 38. 1 *Heb.* 9. And that he hath a name above every name doth evidently appear; for it pleased the Father that in him should all fulnesse dwell, yea, all the fulnesse of the God-head bodily, that in all things, or as it is in the Margent, among all, he might have the preeminence, see *Coll.* 1. 18, 19. 2. 9. so *Phi.* 2. 9. Wherefore (saith the Apostle) God hath also highly exalted him, and given him a name above every name, he hath a name above the Anointed, Kings, Priests, and Prophets of old, they being but types and shadowes of him, and yet were the highest names in *Israel*, which was a Family that had a name above all the Families of the Earth; and so a name above all the names on the Earth : and yet this is not all, for he hath a name above all Principality, and power, and might, and dominion, and every name that is named, not in this world only, but also in that which is to come, *Ephe.* 1. 20, 21, 22. *Phi.* 2. 10, 11.

[*He is the Anointed Priest ; none to, or with him in point of atonement*] That he is the Anointed Priest, compare *Heb.* 3. 1. with 1. 9. and there shall we see the Spirit of God, calling him an High-Priest, who was of God anointed with the oyl of gladnesse above his fellowes, which cannot but be understood of his fellow-Priests, either such as were ordained of old, before the time of Reformation, and so were types, or shadowes of him, or else of such as were since by him made Priests unto God, and so received of the fulness of that his oyntment : Now that there is none to him in point of atonement, will easily be made manifest, if these three things be considered : 1 The nature of the attonement it self. 2 The weaknesse or insufficiency of all other Priests, whether ordained, or made to perform such a work. And lastly, the sufficiency of this High Priest to make a perfect attonement for all those that come to God through him.

Touching the nature of the attonement, it is not amisse to consider, that what was by this word attonement exprest under the first Testament, while that Priesthood stood, hath been since under the administration of the last Testament, that is established upon better promises than that, been exprest more frequently by the word Reconciliation, and therefore the word that in the 5 *Rom.* 11. is rendered attonement, is in 2 *Cor.* 5. 18, 19. and in all other places translated by the word Reconciliation ; Now Reconciliation does pre-suppose an estrangenesse, or enmity rather, between two parties, and if the parties were men, peradventure there might be found a man to mediate ; but the enmity lies not so much between man and man, or between men and Angels, good or bad, but between God and man, the Creator and the creature, and who is he in Heaven, or in Earth, that dare interpose, or step in to make a reconciliation between these two ? yea, who can effect it ? especially if we consider that the enmity on the creatures part is rooted in his mind, and cannot be erad-

icated (I had almost sayd, and yet I think I shall not need
to retract it) by the powerfull hand of God himselfe stretcht
forth in his wrath, his mind still remaining, as indeed doth
notably appear out of the mouth of the Lord himself, by
the hand of his Prophet *Isay.* 57. 16, 17. For the iniquity of his covetousnesse, was I wroth, and smote him;
I hid me, and was wrath, and he went on frowardly in the
way of his heart. So see it confirmed also in *Rev.* 16. 9.
11. 21. When the wroth of God breaks forth with an
exceeding great Plague, then shall you find men blaspheming the name of God, who hath power over those
Plagues, because of their paines and their sores, and repented not of their evill deeds, to give him glory; and if
the wrath of God does it not, how unlike is the wrath of
man to effect it? But further to shew the greatnesse of
the work of Reconciliation as it lies on mans part; for as
he hath not an alienation only, but an enmity in his mind,
so is he apt upon all occasions to the utmost of his power
to manifest the same, by wicked provoking workes against
the God of Heaven, so that let but God himself be manifested in the flesh, or any bright beam of his glory break
forth, and shine through mortall flesh, presently shall the
Iewes, and Gentiles, though otherwise full of enmity one
against an other, concurre; yea, *Herod* and *Pilate* shall
now be made friends, and shall agree to Crucifie the Lord
of Life and Glory; to pour forth the pretious Blood of God,
and to tread under foot the Sonne of God, and to count
the blood of that Covenant as an unholy thing: So that
from hence we may conclude, That as he that hateth his
Brother in his heart may be said to murther a man, so he
that hateth God in his heart, may be said in a sense to
murder God. Now as on mans part there appears such
enmity in his mind, such an aptnesse to vent it, and such
backwardnesse (as I might shew) in him to accept of any,
but especially the Gospell termes of Reconciliation, whereby the work appears to be great; So if we consider it on
Gods part, that the wrath of God is revealed from Heaven,
against all ungodlinesse, and against all unrighteousnesse
of the Sonnes of Men, and that his word is gone forth and
cannot be recalled; In the day that thou eatest thereof,
thou shalt surely dye; and the Soul that sinneth, it shall

dye; and cursed is every one that continueth not in all
things that are written in the Law to doe them, so that his
Wrath, Iustice, and Truth are all engaged in this main
controversie that he hath with his creature, and by reason
thereof, he will not be pleased with thousands of Rams,
nor yet with ten thousand Rivers of Oyl, &c.   And therefore if the question be asked who is worthy, or who is able
to stand between God and Man, to make the attonement,
to slay the enmity, and so to make peace?   The answer
will be the same, That no man (that is meerly so, no nor
Angel) in Heaven, nor in Earth nor under the Earth, is
either worthy, or able to undertake this great work, no
nor in that sense to look thereon; And therefore in the
second place all other Priests will be found insufficient;
for as for the Priests of old, and all that belonged to them,
as Vestures, Vessels, Altars, Temple; and all that was of-
ficiated by them, as their Sacrifices, Attonements, Obla-
tions, blessings, they were too weak to accomplish this
work, for they were not able to make him perfect that did
the service, as appertaining to the Conscience, but brought
their sins to remembrance, instead of blotting them out,
so as to remember them no more, and were indeed but meer
shadowes of good things to come, which they that beleeved
had in their eye, and saw afarre off, see *Heb.* 7. 18, 19.
9. 9. 10. 1, 2, 3, 4, 11. and as for others that are made
Priests unto God, they doe but receive of his fulnesse,
and will readily acknowledge with *Paul*, that through the
Law they are dead to the Law, so as by their own works
or righteousnesse (which now appears to be but glistering
wickednesse, and no other than fruits of that enmity that
was in their minds, by them I say) not to expect to make
their own peace with God; and although it is true they
have liberty to enter into the holiest, yet it is by the blood
of Iesus, and by a new and living way which he hath consecrated for them; and although they may draw neer unto
the holy God with a true heart, and full assurance of Faith,
yet they must have their hearts sprinkled with his blood
from an evill conscience, and their bodies washed with pure
water; and although being in the holy presence of God, they
may, as the Priests of old, offer up prayers with strong cryes
for themselves, and others, yet must they be offered upon

the golden Altar that is before the Throne, and must be mingled, and perfumed with much sweet incense out of the golden censer that is in the Angell of the Covenants hand, and the smoke of the incense must ascend with their prayers before God out of the Angels hand: *Rev.* 8. 3, 4 so that in this point they are nothing, yea lesse, and worse than nothing; but Christ is the very power of God in this point, the substance of all shadowes, and what he did in reference to the work of attonement, and reconciliation, he doth it substantially and effectually, both on Gods part and mans; for he hath both natures in himself, and by reason thereof is an apt Mediator fit to interpose between both to make reconciliation; for he is declared to be the Son of God, wholly without sin, consecrated with an oath of God to be a Priest for that purpose for ever, *Heb.* 7. 21. comp. with 27. 28. who by the eternall spirit of God offered up himself without fault to God his Father, the just for the unjust, so that by one offering, he hath consecrated for ever them that are sanctified, so that there is no more need of offering for sin, see *Heb.* 9. 4. comp. with 10. 14. 18. and is now entred, not into the Holy places made with hands, but into Heaven, to appear in the sight of God for those that beleeve through him, and not with the blood of others, but with his own blood, whereby their consciences are purged from dead works to serve the true and the living God, see *Heb.* 9. 26. 14. yea, and there remaineth, and is set down at the right hand of the throne of the Majesty in the highest,[1] being the mediator of that better covenant, even that which is established upon the best, and absolute free promises, which are to pardon their enmity, and iniquity, and to remember their sin no more, to write his Lawes in their hearts, and to be to them a God, and to undertake that they shall be to him a people; so that as God was in Christ reconciling the world to himself, not imputing their trespasses unto them;[2] so in the ministry of reconciliation Christ is by his Spirit in man shedding abroad the love of God in his heart, and thereby slaying his enmity, by which means he is reconciled to God; so that whom he blesseth, being the High

---

[1] Heb. 1. 3. 8. 1.   [2] Heb. 8. 6. 10, 11, 12.

Priest and Captain of our salvation, shall be blessed indeed; see Acts 3. 26. By all which it doth appear to be a truth, that there is none to him in point of attonement to make reconciliation between God and Man. And now that there is none with him in that great work, neither person, nor service, is also as evident. God the Father hath designed him alone in that businesse, that no Flesh might glory in his presence, see *Acts* 4. 11. 12. 1 *Tim.* 2. 5. *Colloss.* 1. 20. 1 *Cor.* 1. 29. And *Paul* tels the *Galatians* who were about to joyn circumcision, and so works with Christ in this point of acceptance with God, that then Christ should not profit them, and that they were faln from grace, see *Gal.* 5. 23.

[*He is the Anointed Prophet, none to him in point of Instruction.*] That he is the Anointed Prophet, or a Prophet Anointed with the Spirit of Prophecie above his fellow Prophets, and a Teacher immediately sent from God from Heaven, see *Io.* 9. 17. *Luke* 24. 19. *Heb.* 1. 9. *Ioh.* 3. 2. 13. 6. 38. 16. 28.

And that there is no Prophet to him, will evidently appear; for all, the other Prophets of God were such as did bear witness to him,[1] or were types of him, yea *Moses* and *Elias*, those two great Prophets, lay themselves low that he may be exalted; wherefore *Deut.* 18. 15. I (saith the Lord by the hand of *Moses*) will raise them up a Prophet from among their Brethren like unto thee,[2] and will put my words in his mouth, and he shall speak unto them all that I shall command him, and it shall come to pass, that whosoever will not hearken unto my words which he shall speak in my name, I will require it of him. And *Ioh.* 3. 30, 31. He must increase (saith *Iohn* the Baptist, who came in the spirit of *Elias*,[3] and was, saith Christ, more than a Prophet, so that among those that were borne of Women before him there was not a greater[4]) and I must decrease; he that cometh from above (saith he) is above all, he that is of the Earth is Earthly, and speaketh of the Earth, he that cometh from Heaven is above all, and what he hath seen and heard, that he testifieth, and no man receiveth his Testimony; he that hath received

---

[1] *Acts* 10. 43. *Io.* 1. 45.
[3] *Matth.* 17. 12, 13.
[2] *Acts* 3. 21. 7. 37.
[4] *Matth.* 11. 11, 12, 13, 14.

his Testimony hath set to his seal that God is true, for he whom God hath sent speaketh the words of God, for God giveth not the Spirit by measure unto him; and as these great Prophets thus witness to Christ, so the voice that is heard from Heaven by *Iames*, *Cephas*, and *Iohn*, do confirm their testimony, that there is no Prophet to him, for when upon the Mount, *Moses* and *Elias* appeared talking with Christ, and *Peter* would have three Tents or Tabernacles, one for Christ, one for *Moses*, and another for *Elias*, that so no doubt at some times, and in some cases, he might be hearkning to them, immediatly upon the motion, and as an evident manifestation of a dislike thereof, they both vanished, and a cloud overshadow'd them all, and Christ being the Prophet only remaining, there comes a voice out of the cloud which said, This is my wel-beloved Son, in whom I am well pleased, hear ye him; *Mat.* 17. 5, 6, 7. And now that there is none to him in point of instruction, will also appear with respect both to the matter and efficacy. 1 For the matter of instruction, he that cometh from above being also in the bosome of the Father, must needs be above all in his matter of instruction, for what he hath heard and seen in the Fathers bosome, that he Testifies, and speaketh the very words of God, yea declareth and maketh known God himself, being the bright breaking-forth of the Fathers glory, which was that which *Moses*, that great Prophet did so much desire to behold, and could not obtain it; and hence it is, that it is said his hearers were astonished at his Doctrine, concluded no man ever spake like this man, and the best of them knew not whether to go to better themselves, forasmuch as he had the words of eternall life, yea and that holy Spirit of promise which the Saints were and still are to receive, was but to glorifie him, to take of him and his words, and to shew unto them the treasures of light and life, and refreshment that is contained therein; see for the proof of all this, 1 *Io.* 17. 18. *Io.* 3. 31, 32, 34. *Heb.* 1. 3. *Exo.* 33. 18, 27. *Mat.* 7. 28. *Io.* 7. 46. *Io.* 6. 68. *Io.* 14. 26. & 16. 12, 13, 14. And as for excellency of matter, so for efficacy and powerfull instructing, there is none to him in point of instruction, for he it is in whose hand is the Key of David, and he openeth the heart to

understand the scriptures; and to shew a lively experiment
of his powerfull instructing, when he was here upon Earth,
he past by the wise and learned Rabbies, and called the
illiterate and foolish Fishermen, and to this day doth
choose not many wise, nor many learned, but the poor
foolish and despised ones, that as a teacher he may shew
his abilities, thereby giving understanding to the simple,
speaking words of light, and life, and spirit to them, and
by them to confound the wise, and learned, and mighty;
yea he indeed is the light of the Gentiles which sate (and
still in a great measure sit) in darkness, and is that true
light that enlightneth every one that cometh into the
World, see 24 *Luke* 45. 1 *Corinthians* 1. 26, 27. *Iohn* 6.
63. *Acts* 13. 47. *Iohn* 1. 9. And as he was the Prophet,
opening his Fathers Bosome, and shewing the things that
were past and present, so the things also that were to come;
he tells them how many things he must suffer of the Elders,
and Chief Priests, and Scribes, and be killed, and raised
again the third day, and therein foresheweth his Office of
Priesthood; he also foretells how after he is risen as a
Lord, he will set his House in order, and so depart to his
Father to receive his Kingdom, and to return, and what
shall befall his Servants in the time of his absence, by the
reign and rage of the Beast, and Spirit of Antichrist, and
what will be each ones portion at his return, as appears
in the book of the *Revelation*, which is surrounded with
blessings to him that readeth, Chapter 1. 3. and curses to
him that addeth to it, or taketh from it, Chapt. last 18. 19.
Wherefore seeing there is no Prophet or Teacher to Christ
and his Spirit in point of instruction, both for excellency
of matter, and efficacy in teaching, it well suites with
Christians to be still cleaving close to this Prophet, and
concluding with the Disciples that first trusted in him,
Whither shall we go, thou hast the Words of Eternall life.
But to proceed, he is [*The Anointed King, who is gone
unto his Father for his glorious Kingdom, and shall ere long
return again.*] That Jesus of *Nazareth* is the Anointed
King could not be hid in the day of his humiliation, as
appears *Luke* 23. 2, 3. & Chapter 19. 38. The Majesty
of a King did so appear in that lowly and meek form,
while he rode upon an Asse, that if the multitude of the

Disciples had not confest him, but had held their peace, the stones would cry out; yea and then his word had a powerfull efficacy like the word of a King among Men and Devils, the winds and Seas, so that he speaks but the word and the blind see, the lame walk, the deaf hear, the dumb speak, the dead are raised, the Devills are cast out, the poor receive the Gospell; when he is at the weakest, then is *Pilate* forc'd to confess that he is King of the Iews, and to propagate this confession as far as Latin, Greek, and Hebrew will carry it; this appears more evident, since he was raised and sits as Lord at the right hand of the Father, at least in the hearts and lives of his Servants, by powring forth that Spirit or oyntment received, *Acts* 2. 33, 34, 35, 36. So that the Kings of *Israel* were but his types, and the Kings of the Nations are but his Sword-bearers, for he is King of Kings; but most lively shall this truth be made manifest, when all enemies shall become his footstool, and he shall appear indeed in the form of a King with thousands of his Saints, and ten thousand times ten thousand of the heavenly Hosts, and shall in the powerfull word of a King command the Earth and the Sea to give up their Dead, and both wicked men and Devills to go together into torment, and they shall be tormented, and the Saints to enter into the joy of their Lord, and it shall be unspeakably glorious, 25 *Mat.* 31. 32. *Luke,* 9. 26. *John* 5. 28, 29. And that he is gone unto his Father to receive his Kingdom, and shall ere long return again, will be made manifest by these scriptures, *Io.* 20. 17. *Lu.* 19. 12, 13. *Heb.* 9. lust. 2 *Tim.* 4. 1. *Rev.* last, so that as certainly as he hath had a time for his Propheticall Office and for his Priestly, so shall he have a time for his Kingly; and as the dream of *Nebuchadnezzer* hath been found certain, and the interpretation of *Daniel* sure, concerning those four Monarchies or Kingdoms of men which should come to pass in the Earth, so certain and sure it is, that the day is approaching that the God of Heaven will set up his Kingdom by that despised yet Corner-stone that was cut out without hands, *Dan.* 2. 44, 45.

[*That this Iesus Christ is also the Lord, none to or with him, &c.*] That he is the Lord, appears 2 *Cor.* 4. 5. We preach Christ Iesus the Lord, saith *Paul,* and *Acts* 10. 36.

saith *Peter*, he is Lord of all, and hence it is that he is called Lord of Lords. *Rev.*

And that there is none to him by way of commanding and ordering with respect to the worship of God, the houshold of Faith, will evidently appear if the nature of the houshold of Faith, the worship of God, and the commanding and ordering power that suits therewith, be considered with respect unto him. For the nature of the houshold of Faith, they are a company of faithfull ones,[1] that are bought with the price of his blood,[2] knit together in one by his Spirit,[3] founded wholly upon himself, built up by him to be a holy habitation of God,[4] and therefore not in the least measure to be defiled with the inventions and commandements of men,[5] from whence it is that they are still with their ey fixt upon him whom they look upon to be as well the finisher as the author of their faith,[6] still in their hearts calling on him that hath bought them, and saying, Lord what wilt thou have me to doe,[7] and still standing upon their watch to harken what this Lord will speak,[8] for the voice of a stranger they will not hear;[9] so that by this it evidently appears, that there is none that hath so much right unto this houshold of Faith by way of ordering it, nor yet freedom in it by way of commanding, as hath Christ Iesus the Lord; And from the nature of the worship which is spirituall, to be performed by a spirituall worshipper,[10] and after or in that true manner that the Father of spirits hath appointed, it will as evidently appear, that there is none to him by way of commanding and ordering in this matter, who is the only begotten of the Father, came out of, and yet is, in his bosome, and hath declared him, the true way of his worship, and who are such worshippers as he seekes for; who as a Lord faithfull over his house before his departure gave order thereto, commanded his Servants to watch, and to hold fast till he come, and in his absence being at the right hand of his Father, is mindefull to shed abroad of that holy Spirit of Promise, whereby the true worshippers shall be led from truth to truth, untill they be brought into all

---

[1] Eph. 1. 1. Col. 1. 2.
[4] Col. 2. 19. 2 Eph. 20. 21, 22.
[7] Acts 9. 6. [8] Ps. 86. 8.
[5] 1 Cor. 6. 20. 7. 23.
[6] 1 Cor. 3. 16, 17.
[9] Io. 10. 5.
[5] 1 Cor. 12. 13.
[6] Heb. 12. 2.
[10] 4 Jo. 23, 24.

truth. And if the nature of the commanding and ordering power, that suits both with the worship, and with the worshippers, which the Father of Spirits seeks for be also considered, which is not a law of a carnall commandment seconded with carnall weapons, or an arm of flesh: but a spirituall law, or as the Apostle cals it, *Rom. 8. a law of the Spirit of life from Christ Jesus,* spoken unto, or rather written in the heart of a Christian by the Spirit of Christ, by reason whereof he obeyes from the heart, readily, willingly and cheerfully that form of doctrine which is engraven and laid up therein, *Heb. 8. 10. 2 Cor. 3. 2. Rom. 6. 17.* If this I say be considered, that the worship is spirituall, such as must begin in, spring up, and rise from the heart and the spirit, and so be directed to the Father of spirits, and so the commanding power that suits herewith, must speak to the heart and spirit of a man, then is there no Lord in this matter to Christ Jesus the Lord, who speaks to the heart in the Spirit, and his words are as commands from the head to the members, which conveigh together spirit and life to obey them, by reason of which his commands are not grievous, for where the Spirit of this Lord is, there is liberty, and they by beholding the glory of the Lord, are transformed into the same Image, from glory unto glory, by the Spirit of the Lord, *2 Cor. 3. 17, 18.*

And that there is none with him, he is the onely Lord, and law-giver of this spirituall building, and so of the spirits in this sense, appears by such scriptures as say, *One is your Lord and law-giver, James 4. 12. Ephes. 4. 5. Mat. 23. 8. 10.* and by such as say, *ye are bought with a price, be ye not therefore the servants of men,* and the Apostles that had greater authority in this point than any men living, yet they acknowledge they had not Dominion over mens faith, and therefore declare this to be the express mind of God, that the servants of this Lord must not strive (as if they were Lords) but be patient, in meekness instructing those that oppose themselves, or as the word imports, that set themselves by covenant in opposition to that living Lord. And whereas it is declared in the testimony, that this houshold of faith was purchased by his blood as Priest, instructed and nourished by his Spirit as Prophet; &c. this will all evidently appear to be true, *Acts 20.28. John 16.*

from the 7. to the 16.   1 *Cor.* 2. 9, 10, 11, 12.   *Rom.* 8.
John 1. 2. 26, 27.   *Rev.* 2. 11. 17. 29.   2 *Thes.* 14, 15.
1 *Cor.* 11. 2. and 1. 7.   And so is the first part of the testimony by the word of God confirmed and justified.

2. [*I testifie that Baptism or dipping in water is one of the
commands of this Lord Jesus Christ.*]   That this commandment of Jesus is by way of dipping, and as it were by
drowning, overwhelming, or burying in water, and not by
sprinkling with water, appears many waies.

1. In that although there be frequent mention made of
that appointment of Christ in his Last Will and Testament, yet is it never expressed by the word that may be
rendred rantism, or sprinkling, but by the word that is
rendred baptism, or dipping.

2. In that the word by which it is so frequently exprest,
doth in proper English signify to dip, to plung under
water, and as it were to drown, but yet so as with safety,
so that the party (as to the manner) may be drowned again,
and again ; see the instance of *Naaman*, he dipp'd himself
seven times in *Jordan*, 2 *Kings* 5. 14. and to this sense of
the word (at least in that place) both the *Greek*, *Latine*,
and *English* Churches agree.

3. In that the phrase (in which there is mention made
of such an appointment of Christ) doth necessarily import
such a thing, and therefore when mention is made of baptizing, there generally followeth that word the preposition
(ἐν) which is commonly translated in, or into, which suits
with dipping, and not the preposition (συν) which signi-
fies with, and so suits with sprinkling.   And therefore it
may be as well rendred, I baptize you in water, and he
shall baptize you in the holy Spirit, *Mar.* 1. 8. as it is rendred *Iohn* did baptize in the wilderness, and in the River
Jordan, verse 4, 5. or that *Iohn* was in the Spirit on the
Lords day, *Rev.* 1. 10. and they were baptized in the cloud
and in the Sea, 1 *Cor.* 10. 2. yea it may as well be rendred,
I baptize, or dip you into water, as it is rendred they were
casting a net into the Sea *Mar.* 1. 16. for the words are the
same, and it would be an improper speech to say *Iohn* did
baptize with the wilderness, and they were casting a net
with the·sea.

4. That this appointment of Christ is by way of dip-

ping, and not sprinkling, appears, in that for the resemblance, and likeness hereunto, the *Israelites* passing under the cloud, and through the sea, where the *Ægyptians* that were their Lords, and commanders, their pursuers, and enemies, that sought their destruction, were drowned, left behind, and seen no more, is by the holy Spirit called a baptism, 1 *Cor.* 10. 1, 2. they were baptized in the cloud, &c. Where observe it is not here rendred with the cloud, and with the Sea, as in the other place, *Mark* 1. 8. with water, because it suits with sprinkling, although the word be the same ; but in the cloud, and in the Sea, which suits with dipping, or overwhelming, and so with the appointment of Christ, they passing through the midst of the red or bloudy Sea on dry land, which stood on both sides as a wall, and being under the Cloud, were as men in a carnall eie overwhelmed and drowned, and yet truly saved, and safe from their enemies.

5. That this appointment of Christ was not by sprinkling, but by dipping, or putting the person into or under the water, appears by *Philips* baptizing the *Eunuch ;* It is said, *They went both down into the water*, both *Philip* the baptizer, and the *Eunuch* that was the person to be baptized, and being there in the water, *Philip* baptized, or dipped him in that water, as *John* did *Jesus* in the river of *Jordan*, and then it is said as they descended, or went down into the water, so they ascended, or went straitway up out of the water, see *Acts* 8. 38, 39. *Mat.* 3. 16. mark the expression, *And Jesus when he was baptized went up straitway out of the water*, therefore had he been down in the water.

6. That this appointment of Christ was not by sprinkling, but by dipping, or as it were a drowning, appears, in that *Iohn* the Baptizer, his work being to baptize, remains in the wilderness by the river of *Iordan*, and afterward in *Ænon*, and the reason that is rendred by the Spirit of God why there he abode, was, *because there was much water there*, which need not have been, if that appointment could have been performed by sprinkling, and not by dipping. See *Luke* 3. 2, 3. *Iohn* 3. 23.

7. That this appointment of Christ was not to be performed by sprinkling, but by dipping, &c. appears from the nature of the Ordinance it self, for it is such an ordi-

nance as whereby the person that submitteth thereto, doth
visibly put on Christ Iesus the Lord, and is hereby visibly
planted into his death, holding forth therein a lively simil-·
itude, and likeness unto his death ; whereby onely through
faith he now professeth he hath escaped death, and is in
hope to obtain life, and peace everlasting, and so to have
fellowship with him in his death, as to be dead with him,
and thereupon to reckon himself to be dead indeed unto
sin, Sathan, the law, and the curse. See *Gal.* 3. 27. *Rom.*
8. 2. 3. 5. 7, 8. 11. 1 *Cor.* 15. 29. But the planting of a person into the likeness of death, is no waies resembled by
sprinkling; but by dipping it is lively set forth and demonstrated, therefore.

8. This appointment of Christ, *sci.* Baptism, is an ordinance whereby the person that submitteth thereto, doth
hereby visibly and cleerly resemble the buriall of Christ,
and his being buried with him, so as in respect of the old
man, the former lusts and conversation, like the *Egyptians,*
to be taken out of the way, and seen no more. See *Romans*
6. 4, 6. *Col.* 2. 12. But sprinkling doth no way lively resemble the buriall of Christ, or the persons being buried
with him, as dipping doth; therefore.

9. This appointment of Christ, *sci.* Baptism, is an ordinance whereby the person that submitteth thereto, doth
visibly, and lively hold forth herein the resurrection of
Christ, declares him, whose life was taken from the earth,
to be alive again, who although he died and was buried,
yet was he not left in the grave to see corruption, but was
raised again, and behold he liveth for evermore; and as
hereby he holds forth the resurrection of Christ, so doth
he also his own, being planted into the likeness thereof,
so as to reckon himself to be in his soul and spirit quickned, and risen with Christ, from henceforth to live unto
God the fountain of life, and to Christ Iesus the Lord who
died for him, and rose again, and so to walk in newness of
life in this present evill world, being also begotten unto a
lively hope, that in the world to come he shall be raised,
and quickned both in soul, and body, to a life everlasting. See *Rom.* 6. 4. 5. 8. 11. *Acts* 8. 33, 35, 36. *Col.* 2. 12.
Rom. 8. 11. 1 *Cor.* 15. 29. 1 *Pet.* 1. 3. but sprinkling doth
no way lively resemble the resurrection of Christ, or the

souls or bodies rising, or being raised by him, as the way of dipping doth. Therefore this appointment of Christ was, and still is, to be performed by way of dipping or putting the person into or under the water, and not by sprinkling.

And that this dipping in, or into water, in the name of Iesus, is one of the commandments of this Lord Iesus Christ, doth evidently appear *Mat.* 28. 19. *Mark* 16. 15, 16 compared with *Acts* 2. 38. 41. 8. 36. 38. and 10. 47, 48. And that it is also to be observed by all that trust in Christ, as other of his commands, as he is the Lord, untill he come again, is likewise expressly manifested to be his will, *Mat.* 28. 20. *Gal.* 1. 7, 8. *Jude* 3. 2 *Tim.* 2. 2. *Col.* 2. 5, 6. *Rev.* 2. 25. 3. 11. *Hold fast till I come. Rev.* 22. 14. 19. *Heb.* 12. 25. But to proceed.

[*That a visible believer or disciple of Christ Jesus (that is, one that manifesteth repentance towards God, and faith in Jesus Christ) is the onely person that is to be baptized with that visible baptism or dipping of Jesus Christ in water*] That a visible disciple or Scholar of Christ, one that manifesteth himself to have heard him, to have been taught by him, and to have yielded up himself to him as his teacher, is the only person, &c. will be made manifest,

1. By the commission itself, and the argument stands thus, they and they onely have right to this ordinance, and appointment of Jesus Christ, whom the ordainer himself, *sci.* Christ Jesus the Lord, hath in his Last Will and Testament appointed it to; but Christ Jesus the Lord hath appointed it to Disciples, and to Believers, and to such onely. Therefore.

The first proposition cannot be denyed, and the second will easily be proved: see the commission by which the Apostles were warranted to administer this ordinance, and so must all that bap*tise or they will appear but usurpers *Mat.* 28. 18, 19. All power is given unto me in heaven and in Earth, saith the Lord, go ye therefore and discipulize or make disciples not among the Jews only, but among the Gentiles, and Nations, and baptize them; so that if the question should have been made, Lord whom shall we baptise of the Nations among the Jews and Gentiles? his answer was given in the words before, and he would have **given no other, you shall baptize amongst the Nations**

Jews and Gentiles, such as first have been taught, and by teaching have been made my disciples; so *Mar.* 16. 16. Go ye into all the world, saith the Lord, and preach the Gospel to every creature, to the Gentiles as well as the Jews, he that beleeveth and is baptized shall be saved, &c. So that if the question here again should be propounded who among the religious and strict Jews, and the loose and profane Gentiles, should be baptised, the answer is plain, those to whom the Gospel first hath been preached, and they through that Gospel have also believed.

2. By the practice of the Commissioners who were faithful unto their Lord, and to the charge which he gave them, and the argument stands thus.

Such as the faithful Apostles, and first Commissioners of Christ Jesus the Lord administred this ordinance of baptism unto, such and such only ought to be made partakers thereof. But the Apostles and first Commissioners of Christ administred not this ordinance unto carnal babes, infants of daies, such as are by the testimony of the Scriptures declared to be conceived in sin, to be brought forth in iniquity, and being born of the flesh to be but flesh, and so by nature the Children of wrath one as well as another; being also untaught. But to such as first were taught, and were ordained, by the immortal seed of the word, to be born again, and as new born babes in Christ, having tasted of the sincere milk of the word, desire still more of the same, that they might grow up thereby, and such as appeared to be converted and to become as little ones, such little ones as believed in *Jesus*.

The first proposition I suppose none that own Christ and his Apostles will dare to deny. And the second which is more questionable will also be proved. See *Acts* 2. 38, 39, 40, 41, 42, &c. Although *Peter* with the 11 calls upon the convicted Jews to repent, and to be baptized every one in the name of Jesus for the remission of sins, and tells them that then they shall be made partakers of the holy Spirit; and that they should not need to distrust it; he shews them the largeness of the promise that was made concerning the pouring forth of the Spirit, it being promised to be poured forth upon all flesh, as they had exprest in the beginning of their discourse out of *Joel* v. 16. and

17. and therefore saith, tis to you and to your Children, and to all that are afar off, even as many (of you, your children and such as are a far off) as the Lord our God shall call; yet he baptizeth none, but such as were called by the holding forth the word of salvation by Jesus Christ, as appears in the words, for they that gladly received his word were baptized; and they only; for they that were baptized were added, and continued together in the Apostles Doctrine, and in fellowship, and in breaking of bread, and in prayer, and continued dayly with one accord in the Temple, and breaking bread from house to house did eat their meat with gladness and singleness of heart, praising God: all which cannot be understood of infants of daies. And therefore this place if rightly considered will be so far from affording a ground for the baptizing of the children of believing parents, because here it is said the promise is to you and to your children, that it will sufficiently evince the contrary; for indeed such an apprehension is accompanyed with 2 or 3 evident mistakes, there is a mistake in the promise, in the parties to whom the promise belongs, and the manner how it is to them and their children, &c.

1. There is a mistake of the promise, in that it is looked at as the covenant of Grace which doth ingratiate the soul into, and gives it an interest in all the privileges of the Gospel of Christ, and so in order doth go before baptism or any other visible ordinance and appointment of his, whereas in very truth by promise there, is meant that holy Spirit of promise which they which believed in Christ, and obeyed him, should according to promise receive after he was ascended unto the right hand of the father, as appears *Joh.* 7. 39. 14. 16. 16. 7. That which he had here shed abroad in a powerfull manner upon the Apostles, and that which these Jews also in believing and obeying the Gospel of Christ should also receive, and therefore saith *Peter*, repent, and be baptized and ye shall receive, &c. and was no other than that which was of old prophecyed of by *Ioel*, as is declared v. 16. and so is a promise that follows faith and obedience, and not such as goes before to give right to this appointment of Christ.

2. There is a mistake in the parties to whom this

promise belongs, for whereas it is said *to you and to your children*, and thereupon it is conceived to be meant believers, and their infants of daies, which upon that accompt are to be baptized, it is plain and evident when the Apostle spoke these words to them, they could not be looked upon as believers, forasmuch as they being prick'd at the heart, and only convinced of their evill in murdering the Lord of'life, propounded what they should do to be saved, which is farre from believing, to which the Apostle replies, *repent, and be baptized in the name of Jesus for the remission of sinnes;* and to conceive that by their children were meant infants of daies, it may be as well so understood by your Sonnes and daughters, which should so receive of the promise of the Spirit as to prophecy mentioned in the seventeenth verse of this chapter, to which these words are related; and to make it appear that the promise was not so either to them or their children (as yet manifested) to give them right unto baptism, after many more words used by the Apostle to perswade them to save themselves from this adulterous generation, it is said, but as many as gladly received his word were baptized, and but only such, and not their infants of daies, for they that were baptized continued together in such appointments of Christ as infants are in no measure capable of.

3. There is a mistake in the manner how this promise is to them, & their children, not spoken to them now as believers, & their children as having right and interest peculiar by them, but indeed to them, and their children no otherwise than to all that are a far off, which if taken in the generall cannot be understood but with respect to the generall promise, which is to pour forth his Spirit upon all flesh, but if with the restriction, which is, even as many as the Lord our God shall call, then, parents and children, Jews and Gentiles, such as are neer, and as are a far off, must be called by the word of his grace before they can have a peculiar right and interest in this spirit of promise, and so a child that is called to believe and obey the Gospel may have this promise made good unto him before his father, and a Gentile that is a far off before a Jew that is neer.

This will appear also by other instances, as of *Philip*

baptizing in *Samaria,* they were men and women that he baptised there, such as believed and received the word with great joy, *Acts* 8. 8. 12. and when the *Eunuch* seeing the water, asked *what should let him to be baptised, Philip* intimates that although he had been taught, yet the want of a manifestation of faith would be a let, v. 36, 37. And whereas there is mention made of whole houses that were baptised; that the Commissioners might appear faithfull unto their Lord, and keep close to the very words of their Commission, you shall find they were first taught, and by teaching were made his disciples, and gladly received his word. See it in *Cornelius* houshold *Acts* 10. 33, 34. compared with the 44. 47. the *Iaylors* houshold *Acts* 16. 32. 34. *they spake unto him the word of God, and unto all that were in his house, and he set meat before them, and rejoyced, believing in God with all his house ;* see it also in *Crispus* houshold, *Acts* 18. 8, 9, 10, 11. *Stephanus* houshold 1 *Cor.* 1. 16, 17. compared with *chap.* 16, v. 15. And as for *Lydias* houshold *Acts.* 16. the Spirit of God being more silent therein, they that cannot interpret it by the other four, nor yet by the Commission it self, nor by the Commissioners faithful observance thereof in all other instances, let them prove if they can these three particulars. 1. That *Lydia* ever had a husband. 2. In case she had, that ever she had any children by him, and if so, then in the 3. place that they were not dead, or so grown up that they might hear and receive the word gladly as well as their mother.

3. A third argument to prove that a visible believer is the person that according to the mind of Christ is to be baptized in water, may be taken from the order which the Spirit of Christ laies down, faith and baptism, in the scriptures of truth, putting faith still in the first place, witness *Mark* 16. 15, 16. *Mat.* 28. 19. *Heb.* 6. *Eph.* 4. A 4 argument may be taken from the nature of the ordinance, and a 5 from *Johns* Baptism. Yea much more might be said to this point, but this may suffice.

[*And also the only person that is to walk in the visible order of his house, and so to wait for his comming the second time in the form of a Lord and King with his glorious Kingdome according to promise*]

That he is the only person that is to enter into, and walk in the visible order of his house, will evidently appear, if the order in which our Lord left his house when he went to his Father to receive his kingdome be duly considered, for in his last will and testament we shall find it thus recorded, when our Lord was about to be gone, he gave order unto his Apostles, whom he made stewards in his house of the mysteries of God, to make him Disciples of all Nations, and that such as were so made should then be baptized, and so visibly planted into Christ, and put on Christ, and having so received him, should walk in him, observing all things whatsoever he had commanded, the first thing whereof as touching order was, to be added or joined one to another in the fellowship of the Gospel by a mutual professed subjection to the Scepter of Christ, and being a company thus called out of the world, from worldly vanities, and worldly worships, after Christ Jesus the Lord (which is the proper *English* of these words the Church of Christ, and is in other terms called the houshold of faith) should steadfastly continue together in the Apostles doctrine, *sci.* the consolation, reproof, and instruction thereof, in Fellowship, *sci.* mutual support both inward and outward; in Breaking of bread, thereby remembring the death of our Lord, whose soul was made an offering for sin, as his flesh is meat indeed, and his blood drink indeed, by the help of the Spirit, to nourish our souls and spirits up unto eternal life, and in prayer, one with and for another; And that this is the absolute order which the Lord hath appointed in his last Will and Testament, doth evidently appear both by his own precept, and command, and by the practice of such as first trusted in him, and if so, then neither infants of daies, nor yet such as profess themselves to be believers in Jesus, but refuse as a manifestation thereof, according to the practice of such as first trusted in Christ, to yield up themselves to be planted into the death, burial, and resurrection of Christ, and so visibly to put Christ on, as did the Christians of old, I say such have no visible right to enter into, or walk in the order of the Gospel of Christ; and to conclude the point, the argument stands thus. They, and they only,

have visible right to enter into, and walk in the visible
order of Christs house, and so to wait for his comming,
whom Christ Jesus himself being the Lord of the house,
hath appointed, and his Apostles being his stewards, have
approved of; But such as first have been taught and
made disciples or Scholars of Jesus, and believers in
Christ, and afterwards have been baptized or dipped and
thereby visibly & lively planted into the death, burial,
and resurrection of Christ, are they, and they only, whom
Christ hath appointed and the Apostles have approved of.
See his Commission, peruse their practice; *Ergo* They, and
they only, have visible right to enter into, and walk in
the order of Christs house, and so to wait for his comming the second time, in the form of a King, with his
glorious Kingdom, according to promise. See for a far-
ther confirmation of the last clause, in the first Epistle to
the *Corinthians* 1. 7. 1 *The.* 1. 10. 2. *The.* 3. 5. But to
proceed.

[*He is the person that is also to wait for his Lords sending down from the right hand of his father in the time of his
absence the holy Ghost, or holy Spirit of promise, and all this
according to the last will and testament of that living Lord.*]
That this living Lord did promise when he left this present evil world, that is in a great measure subjected to
devils, and went to his Father, not only to return again,
but in the time of his absence (as a testimony of his great
love unto such as are called to be his disciples, & manifest the same by loving him & keeping his commandments, and as a testimony of his loving acceptance at the
right hand of his Father) to send down the holy Spirit,
which should be in them as a well-spring of living water
flowing forth unto eternall life, who being a Spirit of
truth, and sent by Christ who is the truth which God
will exalt, shall glorifie him, take of him and his, and
shew unto them, and so lead them from truth to truth,
until he hath brought them into all truth: as a comforter
or Spirit of comfort, shall fill their hearts with joy in believing, by bearing witness with their spirits, that they
are the children of God, and by revealing unto them the
precious things wch God hath prepared for them that love
him, which neither eye hath seen, nor ear hath heard,

neither hath it entred into the heart of man to conceive;
and as a holy Spirit shall set them apart that are justifyed
by the blood of his Son, unto the holy God, and sanctifie
them throughout in soul, and spirit, and body; and as a
Spirit of supplication shall help them to speak unto God;
and as a Spirit of prophecy to speak unto men: that this
Lord I say did promise unto his disciples, who love him
and keep his commandments, in the time of his absence
the presence of such a Spirit as this, which hath supplies
in him beyond what the soul lacks, and that therefore
they are to wait for this promise, and for these supplies in
his appointments, will clearly appear.

1. Out of the words of the Lord himself.   See *Iohn* 14.
15, 16, 17. so v. 26. *chap.* 15. 26. *chap.* 16. 7, 8. so v. 13,
14, 15. five times in that night in which he was betraied
doth he repeat that promise, to his Disciples that loved
him and kept his commandments, and that he intended
the same unto other visible disciples that should love him
and keep his commandments unto the end of the world,
will also appear; for if the appointment of Christ, *sci.* the
supper that went before, and is exprest chapter the 13.
and the prayer of Christ that followed after, and is exprest chapter 17. did belong unto them that should believe through theirr word till he come again, then this
promise that is so often repeated between, doth as well
belong unto them, as to these; but the former is true;
See *Iohn* 17. 20. 1. *Cor.* 11. 26. therefore the later.

If the consequence be denied, it will still be proved out
of Christs own words; See *Iohn* 7. 37, 38. and the consideration even in reason of Christs exceeding love and tender
care towards all his disciples that love him and keep his
commandments, and their sensible wants of the same
supplies of the Spirit will clearly evince it.

2. It will clearly appear out of the words of the Apostles of Christ; See *Iohns* interpretation of these words of
Christ, *Out of his belly shall flow rivers of living water,*
This spake he (saith *Iohn*) *of the Spirit which they that be-*
lieve on him should receive, for the holy Spirit was not yet,
because Iesus was not yet glorified, John 7. 29.   See also
what they all say with one mouth, after they had received
this holy Spirit with power, whereby they were furnished

as Apostles or Embassadors (of him that had all power in
heaven and earth in his hand) to go forth with the em-
bassage of peace into all Nations, and could deliver the
mind of their Lord unto them in their own language,
Acts 2. 38. 39.   *Repent and be baptized every one of you in
the name of Iesus, for the remission of sins & ye shall receive the gift of the holy Spirit, for the promise is to you, and
to your children, and to all that are a far off, as many* (of
all these) *as the Lord our God shall call, sci.* to repentance
from dead works, to faith in Christ Iesus, to this visible
manifestation thereof by being baptised, and so visibly
planted into the death, buriall, and resurrection of Christ
for the remission of sins.

3. This will also appear by the enjoyments of those
that first trusted in Christ, and visibly manifested their
faith and love in and to the Lord, by keeping his commandments: The Disciples which were also called Apostles, waiting in the appointment of their Lord at *Jerusalem*, received and were filled with that holy Spirit, with
power according to promise.   See *Acts* 1. 4. compared
with 2. 2.   So that great number that were about three
or rather five thousand souls that believed through their
word, were baptised in Jerusalem, and waited in the appointments of the same Lord, that is to say, *together steadfastly in the Apostles doctrine, and in fellowship, and in
breaking of bread, and in prayer*, they also enjoied this
holy Spirit according to promise.   See *Acts* 4. 31.   The
like may be found among the Saints in *Samaria, Acts* 8,
17. in *Ephesus, Acts* 19.   And the same may be found
among the Saints that thus put on Christ, and walked in
him, among those that first trusted in him in all places.
See it in the *Romans* chap. 5. 5. and chap. 8. at large.
See it in the *Corinthians* Epistle 1. chap. 2. 10. 12. and 6.
11. 19. and ch. 12. at large.   In the Galathians ch. 3. 2.
4. 6.   In the *Ephesians* chap. 1. 13.   In the *Philippians*
chap. 3. 3.   In the *Colossians* chap. 1. 8.   In the *Thes-
salonians* Ep. 1. chap. 1. 5, 6. and chap. 5. 19.   This
promise is also found true in the litle children that *Iohn*
writes to, and is often repeated, 1 *Iohn* 3. 24. 4. 13. and
in the 2. 27. he speaks unto them after this manner, *but
the anointing* (speaking of this holy Spirit of promise)

which ye have received of him, abideth in you, and (such is his supply) *that you need not that any man teach you, but as the same anointing teacheth you of all things, and is truth and is no lie, even as it hath taught you ye shall abide in him: And now litle Children abide in him, &c.* And *Iude* telleth us, that the very ground why some that had made a profession of the faith, and order of *Iesus,* caused divisions and offences, contrary to that doctrine they had received, and separated themselves, was, because they were sensuall, not having this Spirit, *Iude* 19. And as all this hath been proved by the last Will and Testament of that living Lord, so is it also clear, that his Will is not to be added to, or taken from, compare *Gal.* 3. 15. with *Rev.* 22. 18, 19. which notwithstanding if any man shall attempt to do, let him know this Lord is alive, and will erelong appear sufficiently able to avenge it.

3. [*I testifie that every such servant of Christ Iesus, may in point of liberty, yea ought in point of duty, to improve that talent which his Lord hath given unto him*] That it is their duty to improve the talent the Lord hath given unto them, and that for that end it was also given, will appear by those two instances of the Lord himself, the first is *Mat.* 5. 13, 14, 15. *Ye* (saith the Lord to his Disciples) *are the salt of the earth, the light of the world, &c. neither do men light a candle and put it under a bushell, but on a candlestick;* whereby he intimates, that if it be far from the intention of men (who are but weak and foolish in their intentions and actions) to light a candle which is for use, and then to put it under a bushell, and so make it useless; then much further from the purpose and intention of God, who is the father of lights, to enlighten the spirit of a man, which is the candle of the Lord, and then to have that light concealed and with-held; therefore it follows, *let your light* (saith the Lord) *so shine before men, that they may see your good works, and glorifie your father which is in heaven.* The other instance is in the 19th chapter of *Luke* 11, 12, 13, 14, 15, 16. to the 27. verse, in which Parable is lively declared by the Lord, 1. That that glorious Kingdome of God that shall certainly appear, should not so immediately appear as some thought it should, for which end is the Parable spoken verse 11.

and the first words of the Parable will prove the same
thing, for the Noble-man (which is Christ Iesus the Lord)
must first go into a far country to receive his Kingdome,
which is to the right hand of the Father, there to sit untill all his enemies become his footstool, and so return.
2. Here is declared the order in which this Lord left this
houshold, when he went to receive his Kingdome, he bestowed gifts or talents upon them, and commands them as
his servants, in their severall places to occupy till he
come, verse 13. which proves that, for which I produced
this Scripture; and for further encouragement unto a
servant of Christ to improve that Talent in his Lords
service that he hath bestowed upon him, 3. In the third
place is declared the exceeding great countenance, and
rich reward which this Lord will bestow upon a faithfull
servant that hath thus improved his Talent, when he
shall have received the Kingdome, and shall return in the
glory of his Father; the countenance (I say) appears in
these words, *he will say, well*, or as it is in the 25 of
*Matthew, well done thou good and faithful servant, thou hast
been faithful in a few things*; the rich Reward appears in
these. *Enter into the joy of thy Lord, or have thou Authority* (in my Kingdom) *over ten Cities, be thou also ruler over
five Cities, &c.* But to proceed.

[*And in the congregation he may either ask for information
to himself*] This was a liberty amongst the *Jews* in their
synagogues or congregations, as appears *Luke* 2. 46.
where Christ being about twelve years old, is found by his
parents among the Doctors, in the Temple, not only hearing them, but asking them questions; and when he also
taught in the Temple, or elsewhere, the people did not
only hear him, but asked him questions, yea made objections against what was delivered, without interruption,
and it cannot be conceived but this is much more a liberty in the congregations, and Churches of Christ; and
therefore 1 *Cor.* 14. 35. where women are directed to ask
their husbands at home if they will learn, and the reason
is given because it is a shame for them to speak in the
Church, it is plainly declared, that men that will learn
may ask in the Church, for it is not a shame for them to
speak there. But to proceed.

[*Or if he can, he may speak by way of prophecy for the edification, exhortation, and comfort of the whole*] by prophecy here I mean a plain, and brief declaration of the mind, and counsel of God, in words significantly and easie to be understood, confirmed by the words of the Apostles and Prophets of God, and brought forth for the edification, exhortation, and comfort of the whole; The 14 of the 1 *Cor.* will plentifully clear this truth, and make this liberty good unto the Saints, in the Churches of Christ, and it cannot be shut out but by the spirit of Antichrist. See *verse* 1. 5. 12. 24. 26. 30, 31. 39, 40. So 1 *Thes.* 5. 19, 20. Quench not the Spirit, is the exhortation to him that is therby moved to speak; and despise not prophecyings, is the exhortation to them that are present to hear. But to proceed.

[*And out of the congregation at all times, upon all occasions, and in all places, as far as the jurisdiction of his Lord extends*] which is not only to the utmost parts of the Earth, but also to heaven. See *Mat.* 28. 18. *Heb.* 1. 2. *Ephes.* 1. 20, 21, 22.

[*May (yea ought to) walk as a Child of light, justifying wisdome with her waies, and reproving folly with the unfruitful words therof, provided, &c.* For a warrant here, see *Deu.* 6. 7. *Mat.* 5. 14. 16. 10. 32, 33. 11. 19. *Eph.* 5. 11. *Act* 4. 20. *Jam.* 3. 13. And so have I done also with the 3d. Conclusion, the fourth followeth.

4. [*I testify that no servant of Christ Jesus hath any liberty, much less authority, from his Lord, to smite his Fellow-servant*] This will be evinced to be a truth many waies from the mouth of the Lord.

1. In that it is the great commandment of this Lord to his disciples, and servants, to love one another, and so to bear one anothers burdens, who ought to have their love stronger than death, so as to lay down their lives for the brethren. See *John* 13. 34. 15. 17. 1 *John* 3. 23. 4. 21. *Gal.* 6. 2. 1 *John* 3. 16. Now to smite one another is a breach of that Law of Love in a very high degree. Therefore.

2. The servants of Christ are called upon by their Lord to learn of him to be meek, and lowly, and are put thereby into a capacity to be further taught the way, and fear

of the Lord, to increase their joy, and they are such as shall inherit the earth, and also heaven, for they shall find rest for their souls; and this meek, quiet and gentle Spirit is declared by the Spirit of the Lord to be an ornament of very great price. See for a proof of all this *Mat.* 11. 29. 21. 5. *Psalm* 25. 9. *Isaiah* 29. 19. *Mat.* 5. 5. 1 *Pet.* 3. 4. But to smite is an argument of a domineering, proud, and lofty spirit, which is far from a Spirit that is meek and lowly. Therefore 3. The servants of Christ are called upon by their Lord to be so far from smiting their fellows, that in case they should be smitten by others for his, and the Gospels sake, meerly on one cheek, they should rather turn the other, than seek to revenge it. See *Luke* 6. 20. *Rom.* 12. 17. 1 *Cor.* 6. 7. *why do ye not rather take wrong* (saith the Apostle) *why do you not rather suffer your selves to be defrauded?* but this is far from smiting one another. Therefore, &c.

4. This Lord being also that Prince of Peace, doth so far dislike such practices as these among any servants of his, that belong to his house, that he hath absolutely and expressly declared, that he by no means will have a striker to supply the Office of an Elder, or Steward therein, no nor one that is of a Lordly, or domineering spirit, nor yet one that is froward, and will be soon angry. See in the first Epistle of *Timothy* 3. 3. *Titus* 1. 7. *Peter* 5. 3. Therefore, &c.

5. That no servant of Christ hath such authority from his Lord to smite his fellows, doth plainly appear in that Parable *Mat.* 18. 34. where it is said, *The Lord was so wroth that he will have that wicked servant delivered to the tormentors,* that did but take his fellow by the throat; and him that fell to smiting his fellowes in his Lords absence: *Mat.* 24. 51. it is said, *The Lord shall come upon, in a day when he looked not for him, and in an hour that he is not awar of, and shall cut him asunder, and appoint him his portion with the hypocrits, where shall be weeping, and gnashing of teeth.* But to proceed in the testimony, where it is said,

[*No nor yet with outward force, or arm of flesh to constrain, or restrain anothers conscience, nor yet his outward man for conscience sake, or worship of his God, &c.*] That this is a truth will be made out by the Scriptures of truth, and that many waies. The first argument to prove it standeth thus.

1. *Arg.* If any Servant of Christ Jesus (be he high, or low, rich, or poor,) have any such liberty, or authority from his Lord so to do, then he is able to shew it, (as that which may be his warrant so to act) either out of the words of the Lord himself, or out of those that were spoken, or writ by the Apostles, which were his Ambassadors, and were furnished from their Lord with commands for his Servants observance until he come again.

But no servant of Christ (I suppose) is able to shew, either out of his own words, or out of the words of the Apostles, any such liberty or authority from the Lord, as that which may be his warrant so to do. Therefore.

The first Proposition cannot be denyed, which is this, If any servant of Christ Jesus have any such authority from his Lord, he is able to shew it, either out of his own words, or from the Apostles. And indeed for a man to act in the name of the Lord, and not to have a word, or warrant from him, is high presumption, and so will it appear if these things be considered.

1. In that it is plainly declared, *That all power in heaven, and in earth, is given unto Christ,* and therefore must all authority in heaven, and in earth, be derived from him; and hence it is, that it concerns the feet and the toes of that great image, if it be possible, to stand clear of him who is that little stone cut out without hands, and shall ere long become a great mountain, and fill the Earth.

2. In that it is as plainly declared, that the living God hath in these last daies spoken by Christ, *Heb.* 1. 1. hath made him the heir of all things, and thereupon hath called upon every one that hath an ear to hear him, hath threatned that soul that will not hear him that he shal be cut of; therfore it concerns every servant of his to take heed he use no such authority over another which he hath not heard and received from Christ.

3. In that it is declared that Christ Jesus the Lord is that one law-giver, and that they are blessed that do his commandements, yea, so blessed, that the Apostle saith he

is become the author of eternall salvation to those that
obey him, and that he is also the Judge unto whom the
living God, hath appointed a great, and notable, and ter-
rible day, in which and by whom he will *Judge the world
in righteousness,* yea, the very secrets of mens hearts, according to his gospel. See *James* 4. 12. *Rev.* 22. 14. *Heb.*
5. 9. *Acts* 10. 42. and 17. 31. *Rom.* 2. 16. From which
consideration it also appears, that it concerns the servants
of Christ, that they despise not such a Law-giver and such
a Judge as he is, in taking such liberty, or exercising
such authority, over other mens consciences, which cannot
be made out from his words that he hath given them; all
which, as so many arguments, will prove the first proposition.

And as for the second, which is this, *sci.* No servant
of Christ can shew a warrant from Christ for such
an authority, either out of his own words, or his Apostles;
if that be denied, we must then call for the warrant,
which must be shewed either out of the Evangelists, the
book of the Acts of the Apostles, the Apostles Epistles,
or the Revelation of Jesus: but I suppose it cannot be
shewn out of any of these. If the 13. of the *Romans* be
produced for a warrant, no man can deny that the power
there spoken of was such as belonged to a heathen, and I
think no man will acknowledge that he had such an
authority from Christ to order mens consciences, or outward man, with respect to the worship of God, and therefore that word cannot be their warrant.

If the words of *Paul,* *Gal.* 5. 12. I would they were cut
off that trouble you, be produced for a warrant, let the
words be considered (and in the first place) there is no
mention made of outward force, or outward affliction, and
therefore no warrant for any outward or carnall hand so
to afflict; but 2. Tho words were spoken to the Churches
in *Galatia,* which were spirituall societies, and concerning spirituall transgressors, and therefore their cutting off
must be from that spirituall relation and union which
hitherto they enjoyed, and how that is done, compare
3. *Acts* 23. with *Mat.* 18. 8. 17. *Rom.* 11. 17. 19. 20. 22.
And the carnall cutting off from the carnall *Israel* (before
the time of reformation) was but a type of this spirituall

cutting off and casting out from the spirituall *Israel* of God since.

And thirdly, consider, the words were spoken by the Apostle *Paul*, who would have us to know (as he declares it, 2 *Cor.* 10. 4.) that the weapons of his warfare were not carnall, he was not wont to strive with them that opposed themselves with carnall weapons, and therefore if he speaks to such persons as these *Galatians* were (that had received such power from the Lord) touching a cutting off, which is a business that belongs to a sword, it would be too carnall an understanding of the place to conceive that this should be done by any other sword, than by the sword of the Spirit, which is the word of God, and can reach to their Spirits, and is the only offensive weapon the Saints are to take in such cases as this against their spirituall opposers; and so have I done with the first Argument. A second, to evince this, is taken from that law wherewith Christ Jesus, that Sonne of Righteousness, hath more or less enlightened the Nations, which I may therefore call the law of Nations, being that law by which the Lord will Judge those which may otherwise be said to be without law: the Law is this, Do, as thou wouldst be done unto, which is also (as Christ speaks) the Law and the Prophets. The argument standeth thus.

2. *Arg.* If every servant of Christ Jesus have a commandement from his Lord, as he will answer it before him when he shall appear as Judge, to do to others, as he would have others to do unto him; then no servant of his can have either liberty or authority from him thus to force another mans conscience, or his outward man merely for conscience sake.

But every servant of Christ hath this command from his Lord, *viz.* Do to others as ye would that others should do unto you. Therefore, &c.

The second proposition is undeniable. See 7. *Mat.* 12. *Luk.* 6. 31. The consequence of the first proposition can scarce be denied, but if any should rashly deny it, then I appeal to that mans conscience, not being seared, which also knows but in part, in the sight & presence of God, whether he can be willing that another who is further informed in the things of God, and is also stronger than he (whether he can be willing, I say, that he) should by such a force constrain or restrain his conscience, although in smaller differences, but how much less in things that do so vastly differ.

3 *Arg.* The third argument standeth thus.

If Christ Jesus the Lord instructed his servants to be meek, lowly, and gentle, yea, kind and curteous to all; sent forth the chiefest of them, and told them that they should be as lambs in the midst of wolves; yea, holds them and us, and all that shall reign with Christ, when he shall appear with his Kingdome, in a continuall expectation of a persecuted and afflicted condition in this present evil world, then it cannot be expected that they should have any such liberty, much less authority, from him thus to persecute, prosecute, or inforce others.

But the first is true. See *Mat.* 11. 29. 1 *Cor.* 13. 4. *Eph.* 4. 34. 1 *Pet.* 3. 8. *Mat.* 10. *Tim.* 2. 3. 12. All that will live Godly in Christ Jesus (saith *Paul*, who well discerned the spirit that was abroad, & that which should remain and increase in the world) shall suffer persecution, and the servant is not greater than his Lord; saith Christ, *Mat.* 10. 24, 25. So that by this it appears, that the first is true, and therefore the second which is this, *That no servant of Christ can expect any such liberty or authority from his Lord thus to persecute, prosecute, or inforce others.*

A Fourth argument against forcing men against their consciences, in the things, and worship of God, is taken from the nature of the conscience of man, and of the worship of God, which are both spiritual; and it standeth thus.

4. *Arg.* That which the Lord hath reserved in his own hand, and hath intended to mannage as part of his own Kingdome by his own power or Spirit, and by another manner of ministery, and sword, than that which is put forth in the Kingdoms of men, his being such as suits with the understanding and conscience of man, as it's a spiritual thing, and with the worship of God, which is also spiritual, that, I say, can no servant of Christ have authority from him, by an other sword, or arm of flesh, to undertake, mannage, or think to effect.

But the Lord hath reserved this great work of ordering the understanding, and conscience, which is the spirit of man, by way of constraint, or restraint; and also the outward man, with respect to the worship of God, I say, he hath reserved this great work, in his own hand, and in the hand of the Spirit, and hath intended to manage it as a part of his Kingdome, by his own Spirit, and by another manner of ministery, than that which is put forth in the Kingdoms of men. Therefore, &c.

The first proposition, I judge, cannot be denied, because if it be by him reserved in his own hand and power, then by his authority it cannot be in the hand of another; and if intended by him to be mannaged by another manner of ministery and sword, than that which is put forth in the Kingdomes of men, then not by the same.

And as for the second, it will appear to be a truth by these following testimonies.

1. That the great work of ordering the understanding and conscience, which is the spirit of a man, by way of constraint or restraint; and also the outward man, with respect to the worship of God, is reserved (as a part of his Kingdome, the spirits of men being the throne of the Lord) in his own hand, and in the hand of the Spirit, doth appear. *Luke* 17. 26. *Rom.* 11. 32. *Isa.* 45. 22. *Zach.* 4. 6. *Prov.* 2. 6. *Iam.* 1. 5. *Io.* 1. 9. *Luke* 24. 45. 2 *Cor.* 4. 6. *Eph.* 1. 18, 19. *Acts* 2. 47. 11. 21. And

2. That he hath intended to mannage it by another manner of sword, or ministery, than that which is put forth in the Kingdoms of men, is also evident, in that he did neither speak to, nor yet make use of the Kings of the earth to make him disciples, nor yet call for their sword to constrain them or others to the worship of God, or to restrain them from their own, although it was performed to dumb Idols, and so unto devils; but made use of the sword of the Spirit, which is his own word, & the ministery of his Apostles, and servants, to hold it forth to the world, and thereby were disciples made unto him, and so by him brought from their own to the worship and service of God. See *Io.* 16. 8, 9, 10, 11. 26. *Acts* 15 16. 18. 1 *The.* 1. 8, 9. ch. 2. 13. *Heb* 4 12.

The fifth Argument against forcing mens consciences,

or rather the outward man for conscience sake in the worship of God, standeth thus.

5. *Arg.* That which presupposeth one man to have dominion over another mans conscience, and is but a forcing of Servants, and worshippers upon the Lord, at the least, which he seeks not for, and is the ready way to make men dissemblers and hypocrites before God and man, which wisemen abhor, and to put men upon the profaning the name of the Lord, that can no servant of Christ Jesus have any liberty, much less authority, from his Lord to do.

But by outward force to seek to constrain, or restrain an others conscience in the worship of God, &c. doth presuppose one man to have dominion over another mans conscience, and is but to force servants, and worshippers upon the Lord, which he seeks not for, and is the ready way to make men dissemblers and hypocrites, and to put them upon the profaning the name of the Lord. Therefore, &c.

The first proposition is undeniable, because it is evident that it is not the will of the Lord that any one should have dominion over another mans conscience ; no not such as had the largest power and presence of the Spirit of God, and the largest interest in the hearts of his people, as had the Apostles, Elders, and Brethren : See 1 *Cor.* 8, 11, 12. 10. 29. 1 *Pet.* 5. 3. *Phil.* 3. 15. 2 *Cor.* 1. 23, 24. & chap. 4. 5. for this indeed would be to enter upon the throne of Christ, to sit in the Temple of God, and is the very highest design of the spirit of Antichrist. See 2 *Thess.* 2. 4. 1 *Cor.* 3. 10. And for any man to enter upon the throne of Christ to set a foot into the Temple of God, is to defile it, and he that defiles the Temple of God, (saith the Apostle) him shall God destroy. And for a man to put servants and worshippers upon the Lord, when he would not have others to put servants upon him, and make men dissemble, when if he be a wise man, he cannot but hate dissembling, must needs be much more abomination to the Lord, so that the first proposition (as I said) cannot be denied.

The second will easily be proved in each particular thereof. As

1. This forcing of all to conform in the worship of God,

doth presuppose one man to have dominion or Lordship over another mans conscience, for who knows not that the worship of God is a case of conscience, and that that worship and service that is pleasing to him, must have the spirit and conscience the chief in it? and therefore, that man which by outward force would cause others to conform in point of worship, must pre-suppose to have power over his spirit and conscience, to cause it to conform likewise, or else he cannot attain unto his Religious intent.

2. This is but a forcing of servants and worshipers upon the Lord, and I say at the best, for it is more likely to force worshippers from him; And this will cleerly appear, because the true worshipers, and such as the father seeks for, are such as worship him in Spirit, and in Truth: See *John* 4. 23, 24. who having received from Christ the Spirit of life and love, have his word stand in their heart, as the word of a King, so that thereby they become a willing people to do him service, and stand not in need of such outward force to compell them thereto; they therefore that stand in need to be, and therefore are by outward force compelled to the worship of God, to the faith and order of the gospel of Christ (they I say) are such servants, and worshipers, as are forc'd upon the Lord, whom he seeks not for.

This outward forcing men in the worship of God, is the ready way to make men dissemblers and hypocrites before God, and men which wise men abhor; the truth of this will be thus demonstrated; for if they be spirituall, true, and willing worshipers, such as the Father seeks for, then what need is there of a constraint or restraint? such are a law of life to themselves; but if they be not, then what make they there before him, who calls for the heart, and wisheth men to look to their spirits, for he is a Spirit, and will be sanctified of all those that draw neer unto him? See *Prov.* 23. 26. *Mal.* 2. 15. *Rev.* 10. 3, 4. Then as they are forced upon the Lord against his will, and without any warrant from him, so are they also against their own, and therefore although their bodies may be present, and through fear of the stroke, or hope of reward, may seem to conform, yet their hearts and

minds not being changed (and the strong holds thereof
not being beaten down, as by such carnall weapons they
are never likely to be) they I say, are absent, and far from
the Lord; so then, while their hearts, and consciences,
still cleave to their Idols, and yet their bodies are caused
to conform, what is this but to make men dissemblers and
hypocrites before God and man? and that it is the way to
put men upon the profaning the name of the Lord, is also
evident; understand by name his attributes, word, ordinances, worship, they are all profaned by such a person
that stands in need to be forc'd to Religion. See *Hag.* 2.
13, for him to call upon the name of the Lord, is to profane the name of the Lord, for their prayers are abomination to him, *Gen.* 4. 26. *Prov.* 28. 9. *Isay* 1. 13. And a
calling the name of God or Christ upon such, is counted by him a blaspheming his name. See *Rev.* 2. 9. 13.
1. 5, 6. and unto the wicked saith God, *Psal.* 50. 16.
*What hast thou to do to declare my statutes, or to take my
Covenant in thy mouth, Seeing thou hatest instruction, and
castest my words behind thee?* By all which it doth evidently appear, that the second proposition doth also stand firm.

A sixth argument against the forcing of men against
their understandings and consciences, is taken from the
prohibition of Christ, and stands thus.

6. *Arg.* If Christ Iesus the Lord hath expresly forbidden his servants by such a force to seek to constrain or
restrain another mans conscience, or his outward man
against his understanding and conscience, in things appertaining to God, although his understanding and conscience be cleerly discerned to be erronious and evil, then
can no servant of Christ Iesus have any liberty, much less
authority, from him so to practise; This cannot be denied.

But Christ Iesus the Lord hath expresly forbidden his
servants so to practise, and for the proof hereof, take two
or three instances, *Mat.* 15. 14. where Christ speaking to
his disciples, touching the Pharisees, who were blind
guides, seducers, hypocrites, strong opposers of Christ, yet
seemingly full of zeal and devotion, and such as brought
a vanity upon the worship of God, and made his commandements of none effect by their traditions, as appears,
v. 3, 4, 5, 6, 7, 8, 9. of the same chapter, yet v 14. saith

Christ to his disciples, let them alone, they are blind, leaders of the blind, and so leaves them to that sad event, which is, their falling into the ditch, or perishing together.   See the parable of the wheat and the tares, *Mat.* 13. 24. interpreted by Christ himself, v. 37, 38.   *And he that soweth the good seed* (saith Christ) *is the Son of man, The field is the world, the good seed are the children of the Kingdome* (which being sown by the son of man, must needs be meant faithfull and sincere-hearted proffessors of the truth of the gospell:) *But the tares* (saith he) *are the children of the wicked one, and the enemy that soweth them is the devill*, which being the children of the wicked one, and sown by the devill after the children of the Kingdome, must needs be meant such as crept in unawars, and were sent in as *Paul* speaketh, See *Gal.* 24. to spie out the Saints liberties, that they might bring them into bondage, and so were formall Professors of Christ at the first, but afterwards discovered to be Hereticks, Schismaticks, Apostats, Blasphemers, such as was *Hymintus, Phyletus, Alexander, Demas*, and such false teachers as *Peter* speaks of, 2 *Pet.* 2. 12. *That should bring in damnable heresies, even denying the Lord that bought them*, and bring upon themselves swift destruction, whose pernicious wayes many should follow; by reason of whom the way of truth should be evill spoken of: but to go on, *the harvest*, saith Christ, *is the end of the world, and the reapers are no other than the angels;* Now the question (for our instruction in righteousness) being made by the servants unto their Lord, when the tares were discovered, whether it was his will that they should go and gather them up, and take them out of the field, his first answer, v. 29. is nay, and the reason he renders, is this, *lest while ye gather up the tares, ye root up also the wheat with them;* And the next answer, v. 30. is an express word of command, *that they should let both grow together in the field*, which is the world, and untill the time of the harvest, which is the end thereof, and then his purpose is to speak to the reapers, which are not men but Angels, to gather them up, and bind them in bundles to burn them.   I shall produce but one instance more to shew that our Lord Jesus forbids such a practice as this among his Disciples or servants, 2. Tim. 2. 24, 25,

26. *The servant of the Lord*, saith *Paul*, in the word of the Lord, *must not strive, but be gentle unto all men, apt to teach*, not to strike, *patient in meekness, instructing those that oppose themselves;* which word signifieth a setting a mans selfe in an opposition to the truth in a more than ordinary manner, even by way of covenant or resolution of spirit, yet are they still to be waiting with meekness upon them, *if God at any time will give them repentance to the acknowledgement of the truth, that they may recover themselves out of the snares of the devil, who are taken captive by him at his will.*

Another argument that there can be no warrant from Christ for such a practice as this, is taken from such expressions of his, whereby he shews his dislike thereof, and it standeth thus.

7. *Arg.* If Christ Jesus the Lord have sharply reproved and checked his servants when he hath espied such a spirit as this but breaking forth in them, then can no servant of his have any countenance, much less authority from him so to practise. But the first is true, he hath sharply reproved them when he espied such a spirit as this but breaking forth, witness his words *Luke* 22. 24. 25. &c. *Joh.* 18. 10. 11. *Mat.* 26. 51. 52, 53, 54, & *Luke.* 9. 46. 47. & 49, 50. & 52, 53, 54. 55. 56. where it is said, when the *Samaritans* perceived that Christs face was towards *Ierusalem* they did so envy him for *Ierusalems* sake, which was the place of Gods worship, that they would not receive him nor afford unto him such common curtesie as belonged unto strangers, for which discurteous repulse of their Lord and master, *James* and *Iohn* in a preposterous zeal judged, that they deserved to dy, and thereupon moved the question to Christ in these words, verse, 55. *Wilt thou that we command fire to come down from heaven and consume them?* but what is the answer of Christ? it is said, *he turned, and rebuked them, saying, ye know not what manner of spirit ye are of.* They were scarce awar that they were hereunto moved, by no other spirit than the spirit of Antichrist, for saith he, *The Son of man is not come to destroy mens lives, but to save them*, and if he came into this world to save mens lives, and not to destroy them, and will have his Servants to learn of

him meekness, and mercy, and to be as he was in this
present evil world, I say, if he came to save mens lives,
even the rebellious, then no servant of his can have any
authority from him for such cases as these to destroy them.

The last Argument standeth thus.

8. *Arg.* That which of it self is inconsistent with the
civil peace, liberty, prosperity and safety of a Place, Commonwealth or nation, no servant of Christ Jesus can have
liberty, much less authority from his Lord to do. But
this outward forcing of men in matters of conscience towards God to believe as others believe, and to practise
and worship as others do, cannot stand with the Peace,
Liberty, Prosperity, and safety of a Place, Commonwealth,
or nation. Therefore no servant of Christ can have any
liberty, much less authority so to doe.

The first proposition can scarce be denyed if these
things be considered *sci.* That Christ Iesus the Lord is
the Prince of Peace, *Isa.* 9. 6. *Heb.* 7. 2. and the more a
man is made partaker of, and led by the Spirit of the
Lord, which is the Spirit of Peace, the more peaceable
and quiet is he like to be towards all those with whom he
hath to do, for this Prince of Peace hath given express
command unto all his Servants, who are the Children of
Peace (in whose hearts his word stands, with power, as
the word of a King) to be at peace among themselves,
1 *Thes.* 5. 13. *To love in peace.* 2 *Cor.* 13. 11. *To follow
peace with all men, Heb.* 12. 14. *To seek peace and ensue
it,* 1. *Pet.* 3. 11. *To follow after those things that make for
peace, Rom.* 24. 19. *If it be possible as much as in them
lyeth to have peace with all men,* Rom. 22. 16. *Yea not to
seek their own, but every man anothers wealth,* 1 *Cor.* 10.
24. *To seek the peace of the place, where God hath bounded
his habitation, yea, and to pray unto God for it, and for the
rulers thereof, Jer.* 29. 7. 1. *Tim.* 2. 2. By all which it
doth evidently appear, that that which of it self cannot
stand with the peace and prosperity of a place, and nation,
that can be servant of Christ have by the authority of
this Lord, unless by a just judgement from him upon the
rulers of this world for giving their power, and sword, to
the beast, thus to be chused and made drunk with the
blood of the Saints, which his tender heart cannot but

avenge upon themselves, and upon the Nations for their
loving to have it so.

And as for the second Proposition, which is this, that
this outward forcing of men in matters of conscience towards God to believe as others believe, and to practise
and worship, not as themselves (but as others) are perswaded cannot stand with the peace, liberty, prosperity,
and safety of a Place, Nation, and Commonwealth; this
will as plainly appear in the examination of each particular thereof.

And first, it cannot stand with the peace of a Commonwealth, for as there could be no peace expected in the
Israel of old, so long as that harlot *Jezabell* (who thirsted
after innocent blood) could at her pleasure obtain the seal
and power of the King, to effect her bloody design upon
the servants of the Lord, who withstood her Idolatrous
Priests, and that Idolatrous way and worship which they
had set up, so likewise as long as that spirituall *Jezabell*
among those that account themselves the *Israel* of God,
(who is seen in *Rev.* 17. 3. to ride upon that scarlot-col-
oured beast, and to own herself as the City and spouse of
that great King, the King of Saints, so long I say as she,
can by her glorious deckings and splendours, so deceive
and allure the Kings and Rulers of the earth, to commit
fornication with her, and to give their sword and power
to the beast that bears her up, there can be no expectation of peace in the earth, but still of wars, and rumors of
wars, untill mens hearts fail them: for so long as there is
an outward force or power to be had to maintain and uphold the carnall interests and advantages of some upon
religious accounts, and so prosecute others, who for conscience sake towards God, dare not, yea cannot conform
to their way. What hopes are hereby begotten and
nourished in some? what jealousies, suspitions and fears
in others? what revengefull desires in most? yea, what
plottings and contrivings in all? and as a fruit and effect
hereof, what riding? running? troublesome, and tumultu-
ous assemblings together, and sidings? yea, and outra-
gious murderings and bloodshedings are hereby produced
in a Nation, to gain that power and sword to their party,
either to crush, suppress, or cause the other to conform, or

at the least and best to save themselves from being crushed, suppressed or forced to conformity?   But were this snare of the destroyer and murderer once discovered and broken, which is under a specious and religious pretence of doing God good service, to oppress and slay his innocent servants and children, and to force men to that which their minds and consciences are not perswaded unto, which is worse than Idolatry; or at least would it please the most high to help the Kings and Rulers of the earth, to take King *Davids* counsell, *Psal.* 2. which is, *to kiss the son lest he be angry, and in his anger smite that glorious Image,* (which *Nebuchadnezzar* saw in his dream) Dan. 2. 31, 32, 33, 34. upon his feet, that were part of iron, and part of clay, and so break them to peeces, that the iron, the clay, the brass, the silver, and the gold be broken to peeces together, become as chaff, and so vanish away, that there should no place be found for them; And would it please the most high to put it into their hearts, to manage that power and sword of steel which he hath put into their hands (and takes out again at his good pleasure) so that it might onely attend the very thing for which it is bestowed upon them, which is to do justly, and to shew mercy, as those that walk (in such eminent places) humbly before the Lord, which are things more pleasing to him, then such burnt offerings and sacrifices, although they amounted to thousands of rams, or ten thousands of rivers of oyl, especially being such as he hath not required at their hands, how soon would the earth which now is moved exceedingly, reel to and fro like a drunkard, and is removed like a cottage, become a quiet and peaceable habitation, for if there were neither fear on one hand, nor hope on the other, that this sword should be drawn forth to maintain the carnall interest of some, which they enjoy upon religious pretences, and to suppress the understandings and consciences of others, to the hazard of their proper and lawfull interest and outward enjoyments, and all men should see the Rulers as resolute in this point as *Galle* was, so that men of all sects and religions, which now are pious, were become hopeless of any other help to support themselves and their way, or to draw others thereto, than what by the word of God they can attain unto, how soon would these tumults cease, the enmity in point of Religion be slain, and all things be in peace? and for my part I cannot expect that the swords should be beaten into plowshares, and spears into the pruning-kooks, that nation shall not rise against nation, neither shall they learn war any more, which is a thing which the mouth of the Lord hath spoken of, untill that be accomplished which should occasion it, which is [expressed] by the Prophet in these words, *For all people will walk every one in the name of his God, and we will walk in the name of the Lord our God forever and ever.* Micha. 4. 3, 4, 5.

And as his forcing of men for their conscience sake, cannot stand with the peace of a Nation or Commonwealth, so neither can it stand with the liberty thereof, as those two instances *Rev.* 13. 10. and 15. 16, 17, together with daily experience, doe lively demonstrate, in which Scriptures it is plain to be seen, that whilst the Beast reigneth, through the power of the Kings of the Earth, all are restrained of their liberty, and brought to conformity, they cannot buy nor sel, unless they conform to the Beast, no not the great ones. Kings and Rulers themselves, they shall rather cease to be Kings than cease to conform, when once they have given their power to him, for then they have not been able to stand before him, as Emperors, Kings, Princes and Governors have by wofull experience (through a sad hand of God) found to be true. And as by the righteous judgement of God, they that have upon this accompt killed with the sword, must have a time also to be killed with the sword; so they that have led into captivity, must also be led into captivity; so that by this it appears, it cannot stand with the liberty of a place and Nation.

And that it cannot stand with the prosperity and safety therof will appear from a twofold consideration, the first whereof is with respect to piety, the second to policy.

That which is taken from piety is this, If the matter be duly considered and weighd, it cannot be expected but that this outward constraint or restraint of men in matters of conscience, & for the worship of God (in this present evill world, and by the powers therin) must chiefly

reflect, and light upon such as being called out of the
world, can neither conform to worldly vanities, nor worldly worships, but to the pure voice and word of God, and
to the testimony of Christ Jesus the Lord, which if true,
as indeed it cannot be denied, then it will easily appear
to be both unsafe and unprosperous for a state or nation
to be found medling herein, for as much as the Lord of
hosts hath said, *he that toucheth you, toucheth the aple of
mine eye, Zach.* 2. 8. *and again, Touch not mine anointed,
and do my Prophets no harm,* 1 Chron. 16. 22. and King
David had well observed concerning the *Israel* of old, that
the Lord suffered no man to do them wrong, but even reproved Kings for their sakes, *Psal.* 105. 14.   And if the
Lord of hosts who is full of bowels of compassion, be so
taken with the oppression of the poor, and sighing of the
needy, that he will not long forbear, but will arise, relieve
him, and set him in safety from him that puffeth at him,
or would insnare him, *Psal.* 12. 5. shall he not much
rather avenge his own elect, which give him no rest, but
cry night and day unto him? Luk. 18. 7. yea, I tell you
(saith Christ) he will avenge them speedily.   And now
how unsafe and unprosperous it is for a Kingdome, or
State, to ly thus open to the vengeance of God, which if
it breaks forth is like to overturn, overturn, overturn it as
the prophet speaks, *Ezek.* 21. 25, 26, 27. will not be a
hard thing to discern.

Again it cannot well stand with the prosperity and
safety of a State, or Nation, upon a politick ground or
consideration.   For it best suits with policy (be the power
in the hands of Kings and Princes, but especially of
States and Commonwealths) 1. To engage (not only one
party or sect alone, but) all parties therein to the present
power, and to the supporting thereof.   2. To do this (not
by giving away any part of the power to any party or sect
to oppress or inforce others to their way for their carnal
and private respects, for that (as hath been shown) is the
way to lose it themselves, except they conform, yea to be
brought to conformity, but) to afford its protection equall
to all without respect unto any, at least in this, *sci.* keeping them thereby safe, under God, in respect of their
persons, names, and estates; 3. And to engage them all

upon the strongest engagements, which are not carnal outward advantage, (they being oftentimes so far from advancing the same, that they prove notable means to make the obstruction) but this, wherein one man may be as wel assured that he shall not be forced to another mans understanding and conscience, as that another shall not be forced unto his. Which indeed is an engagement that is stronger than death, the voice of each mans conscience being to him as the voice of his God; by this means shall all parties be deeply obliged to the utmost of their lives and estates, to bear up that power, without which they cannot expect to enjoy peace, liberty, and safety themselves, so shall the rulers also have somewhat more vacancy to consider what it is that the Lord of hosts doth require at their hands, which is to do justly, to love mercy, and to walk humbly before the Lord, *Mic.* 6. 7, 8. And whereas it is added (every man being such &c.) which is to shew that whether such liberty as this should be granted or not in this present world, yet it concerns, and also well becomes the servants of Christ, not to alter their course, but to be still found keeping the commandments of God and the testimony of Jesus, and to be bearing in mind what is said, *Rev.* 12. 11. And they overcame him by the blood of the Lamb, and by the word of their testimony, and they loved not their lives unto the death; harkning also for his voice, who saith *Rev.* last 20. Surely I come quickly, with the like closing therewith as there is exprest. Amen, even so come Lord Jesus.

FINIS.

John Clarke, M.D.

John Clarke, M.D., one of the most eminent men of his time, and a leading spirit among the founders of Rhode Island, was, according to the best authorities, born in Suffolk, England, Oct. 8, 1609. His father's name was Thomas, to whom belonged a family Bible which is still in existence and contains a family record. His mother, Rose Herrige, was of an ancient Suffolk family. The tradition that he was a native of Bedfordshire may have had its rise from the fact that there he married his first wife, Elizabeth, daughter of John Hayes, Esq. To receive a legacy given her by her father out of the manor of Wreslingworth, Bedfordshire, he signed a power of attorney, March 12, 1656, styling himself John Clarke, physician, of London. During his youth he received a careful training, and shared in the intellectual quickening of the period, though at what university he was graduated is not known. His religious and political convictions closely identified him with that large and growing body of men who bravely sought to limit kingly prerogative, and to throw around the personal liberty of subjects the protection of constitutional safeguards. He was indeed a Puritan of the Puritans. All efforts to reform abuses in either church or state proving abortive, he directed his footsteps toward the New World, arriving at Boston in the month of November, 1637.

A bitter disappointment, however, awaited him. The Antinomian controversy had just culminated, and one of the parties was being proscribed. Differences of opinion he expected to find on these Western shores, but he was surprised to find, as he tells us, that men "were not able to bear each with other in their different understandings and consciences as in these utmost parts of the world to live peaceable together." Since the government at Boston was as repressive and intolerant as that from which he had just fled, he proposed to a number of the citizens, for the sake of peace, to withdraw and establish themselves elsewhere, and consented to seek out a place. He had boldly resolved to plant a new colony, and upon a new basis; to incorporated into its foundation principles hitherto deemed impracticable, and even subversive of government, and indeed of all order.

The choice company he had gathered signed, March 7, 1638, the following compact: "We, whose names are underwritten, do here solemnly, in the presence of Jehovah, incorporate ourselves into a Body Politic, and as he shall help, will submit our persons, lives, and estates unto our Lord Jesus Christ, the King of Kings and Lord of Lords, and to all those perfect and most absolute laws of his given us in his Holy Word of truth, to be guided and judged thereby." They found in the Word of God warrant for their civil government, and claimed for it divine authority. It was, nevertheless, "a democracy or popular government," and no one was "to be accounted a delinquent for doctrine." Liberty of conscience was most sacredly guarded. The magistrate was to publish only "breaches of the law of God that tend to civil disturbance." The largest personal freedom consistent with stability of government was provided for. There are good reasons for believing that to the hand of Mr. Clarke this initial form of government must be traced.

The place selected for the colony was an island in the Narragansett Bay, known by the Indians as Aquidneck, but subsequently named Rhode Island, which, Neal says, "is deservedly called the paradise of New England." The lands were obtained by purchase of the aborigines, the deed bearing date 24th March, 1638, the settlers "having bought them off to their full satisfaction." At first established at the north end of the island, the government was, the following April, transferred to the south end, which received the name of Newport. When in 1647 the island was united, under the charter of 1643, in a confederacy with the other towns included in what afterwards became the State of Rhode Island, the government of the united towns was framed by some one on the island. It is generally supposed, and for good reasons, that Mr. Clarke was the author of the government framed, both of the code of laws and of the means of enforcing it. "From the islanders," says Gov. Arnold in his history, "had emanated the code of laws, and to them it was intrusted to perfect the means of enforcing that code." The code, which has received from most competent judges the highest praise, concludes with these words: "And otherwise than thus what is herein forbidden, all men may walk as their consciences persuade them, every one in the name of his God. And let the saints of the Most High walk in this colony without molestation, in the name of Jehovah, their God, for ever and ever."

While constantly busy with the affairs of state. Mr. Clarke did not neglect the higher claims of religion. He is spoken of by early writers as the religious teacher of the people, and as such from the beginning. A church was gathered in 1638, probably early in the year, of which Mr. Clarke became pastor or teaching elder. He is mentioned (in 1638) as "preacher to those of the island," as "their minister," as "elder of the church there." Mr. Lechford writes in 1640, after having made a tour through New England, that "at the island . . . there is a church where one Master Clarke is pastor." On his return to England, he adds, when revising his manuscript for the press, that he heard that this church is dissolved. A report had doubtless reached him of the controversy which had arisen on the island respecting the authority of the Bible and the existence upon earth of a visible church, when some became Seekers and afterwards Quakers. Missionary tours were made in various directions, and numbers were added to the church from sections quite remote, as from Rehoboth, Kingham, Weymouth. Some of them continued to live at a distance. One of these was William Witter, whose home was in Lynn. Becoming infirm he was visited by his pastor, Mr. Clarke, in 1651, who reached his house the 19th of July, accompanied by Obadiah Holmes and John Crandall, elders in the church. The three visitors were summarily arrested, and without there being produced "either accuser, witness, jury, law of God, or man," were sentenced. They were each to pay a fine, "or else to be well whipped." Some one unknown to him paid, it is said, Mr Clarke's fine of twenty pounds. At any rate he was, after a detention reaching into the middle of August, set free as summarily as he had been apprehended. He had hoped for the sake of the truth that there might be a public disputation, his last communication on the subject to the governor and his advisers being dated from prison, 14th August. Though disappointed in this hope, the results of the visit were far-reaching and most gratifying. Many eyes were opened to the truth, and "divers were put upon a way of inquiry."

Meanwhile the colony was in peril, its government in jeopardy, and its very life threatened. On his return from Lynn he was importuned to go to England and represent the infant colony at the English court, and complying with the request, set sail in November, 1651. The following year, 1652, his famous work in defense of liberty of conscience, entitled "Ill News from New England," etc., was published in London. The immediate object of his visit–the revocation of Gov. Coddington's commission–having been attained, he continued to reside abroad to watch over the imperiled interests of the unique State, and succeeded not only in parrying the attacks of enemies, but in gaining for it a substantial advantage over its older and more powerful rivals. The boundaries of the State were even enlarged. The charter obtained in 1663 guaranteed to the people privileges unparalleled in the history of the world. It is an evidence of his skill in diplomacy that he could obtain from King Charles, against the earnest prayers of the older colonies, a charter that declared "that no person within the said colony, at any time hereafter, shall by anywise molested, punished, disquieted, or called in question for any differences of opinion or matters of religion." In the second of two addresses presented to the king he said respecting his colony, that it desires "to be permitted to hold forth in a lively experiment that a flourishing civil state many stand, yea, and best be maintained, and that among English spirits, with a full liberty of religious concernments." To these labors in England his colony was deeply indebted, owed indeed its existence. Yet they have never been duly appreciated, nor have the difficulties environing his way been sufficiently considered. The consummate fruit of his toils– the securing of the great charter–has even been ascribed to another, as indeed have also the results of others of his labors. The charter was received by the colony with public demonstrations of great joy.

His return home in July, 1664, after an absence of more than twelve years, was hailed with delight. He was immediately elected to the General Assembly, and re-elected year by year until 1669, when he became deputy-governor, and again in 1671. During these years he performed much important public service; was in 1664 the chief commissioner for determining the western boundary of the State, and the same year chairman of a committee to codify the laws; two years later he was appointed alone "to compose all the laws into a good method and order, leaving out what may be superfluous, and adding what may appear unto him necessary." Although he retired from public life in 1672, his counsels were still sought in emergencies. Only six days before his death he was summoned to attend a meeting of the General Assembly, which desired "to have the advice and concurrence of the most judicious inhabitants in the troublous times and straits into which the colony has been brought." He died suddenly, April 20, 1676, leaving most of his property in the hands of trustees for religious and educational purposes. His last act was in harmony with one of the first on the colony's records, which was to establish a free school, said to have been the first in America, if not in the world.

He was a man of commanding ability, and from first to last planned wisely and well for his colony. His endowments of both mind and heart were of a very high order. He was "an advanced student of Hebrew and Greek." Arnold says, "He was a ripe scholar, learned in the practice of two professions, besides having had large experience in diplomatic and political life. . . . With all his public pursuits, he continued the practice of his original profession as a physician, and also retained the pastoral charge of his church. He left a confession of his faith, from which it appears that he was strongly Calvinistic in doctrine." His views of Christian doctrine have been pronounced "so clear and Scriptural that they might stand as the confession of faith of Baptists today, after more than two centuries of experience and investigation." He has, and perhaps not inaptly, been called the "Father of American Baptists." And his, it has been claimed, "is the glory of first showing in an actual government that the best safeguards of personal rights is Christian law." Allen (Biog. Dict.) says, "He possessed the singular honor of contributing much towards establishing the first government upon the earth which gave equal liberty, civil and religious, to all men living under it." Backus: "He was a principal procurer of Rhode Island for sufferers and exiles." Bancroft: "Never did a young commonwealth possess a more faithful friend." Palfrey although ungenerous and unjust in his judgments upon Rhode Island affairs and Rhode Island men, and especially toward Mr. Clarke, is constrained to admit that he "had some claim to be called the father of Rhode Island;" and that "for many years before his death he had been the most important citizen of his colony." Arnold says he was "one of the ablest men of the seventeenth century." "His character and talents appear more exalted the more closely they are examined."

William Cathcart
The Baptist Encyclopedia
Pages 227-230

Adlam, Samuel - *The First Church in Providence, Not the Oldest of the Baptists in American, Attempted to be Shown* (Newport, RI: Cranston and Norman's Power Press, 1850)

Backus, Isaac - *A History of New England, with Particular Reference to the Denomination of Christians called Baptists.* 2d ed. with notes by David Weston. 2 volumes. (Newton, MA: Backus Historical Society, 1871)

Bartlett, John Russell, ed. - *Records of the Colony of Rhode Island and Providence Plantations, in New England.* 7 volumes. (Providence, RI: A. Crawford Greene & Brothers, State Printers, 1857-62)

Battis, Emery J. - *Saints and Sectaries: Anne Hutchinson and the Antinomian Controversy in the Massachusetts Bay Colony.* (Chapel Hill, NC: The University of North Carolina Press, 1962)

Bicknell, Thomas W. - *Story of Dr. John Clarke, The Founder of the First Free Commonwealth of the World on the Basis of 'Full Liberty in Religious Concernments.'* (Providence, RI: by the Author, 1915)

Bozeman, Theodore Dwight - *To Live Ancient Lives: The Primitivist Dimension in Puritanism* (Chapel Hill, NC: University of North Carolina Press, 1988)

Bridenbaugh, Carl - *Fat Mutton and Liberty of Conscience: Society in Rhode Island, 1636-1690* (Providence, RI: Brown University Press, 1974)

Callender, John - *Historical Discourse on the Civil and Religious Affairs of the Colony of Rhode-Island and Providence Plantations in New-England in America. From the first Settlement in 1638 to the End of the First Century* (Boston: S. Kneeland and T. Green, 1739)

Cathcart, William, ed. - *The Baptist Encyclopedia.* (Philadelphia: Louis H. Everts, 1881) pp. 227-230.

Christian, James H. - "John Clarke: Baptist Statesman" (Th.D. dissertation., Eastern Baptist Theological Seminary, 1950)

Chapin, Howard M., ed. - *Documentary History of Rhode Island.* 2 vols. (Providence, RI: Preston and Rounds Co., 1916-19)

Chaplin, Jeremiah - *Life of Henry Dunster.* (Boston, MA: James R. Osgood and Company, 1872)

Christian, James H. - "John Clarke: Baptist Statesman." (Th.D. dissertation., Eastern Baptist Theological Seminary, 1950)

Comer, John - *The Diary of John Comer.* ed. C. Edwin Barrows and J. W. Willmarth. Rhode Island Historical Society Collections, Volume 8, (Providence, RI: 1893)

Savage, James, Richard S. Dunn and Laetitia Yeandle, editors - *The Journal of John Winthrop, 1630-1649.* (Cambridge, MA: Harvard University Press, 1996)

Foster, Stephen - *The Long Argument: English Puritanism and the Shaping of New England Culture*, 1570-1700. (Chapel Hill, NC: University of North Carolina Press, 1991)

Gaustad, Edwin S. - "John Clarke: Good Newes from Rhode Island" *The Baptist History & Heritage* 24, No. 4, (October, 1989) pp. 20-28.

Gaustad, Edwin S. - *Baptist Piety: The Last Will and Testimony of Obadiah Holmes* (New York: Arno Press, 1980)

Greaves, Richard L. - "A Colonial Fifth Monarchist?: John Clarke of Rhode Island" *Rhode Island History* 40 (1981)

Gura, Philip F. - *A Glimpse of Sion's Glory: Puritan Radicalism in New England, 1620-1660* (Middletown, CT: Wesleyan University Press, 1984)

Hall, David D., ed. - *The Antinomian Controversy, 1636-1638, A Documentary History.* 2d ed. (Durham, NC: Duke University Press, 1990)

Holifield, E. Brooks - *The Covenant Sealed: The Development of Puritan Sacramental Theology in Old and New England, 1570-1720* (New Haven, CT: Yale University Press, 1974)

Hosmer, James K., ed. - *Winthrop's Journal: A History of New England, 1630-1649.* 2 vols. [Original Narratives of Early American History.] (New York: Charles Scribner's Sons, 1908)

King, Henry Melville - *A Summer Visit of Three Rhode Islanders to the Massachusetts Bay in 1651.* (Providence, RI: Preston and Rounds, 1896)

LaFantasie, Glenn W., ed. - *The Correspondence of Roger Williams.* 2 volumes. (Hanover, NH: University Press of New England of the Rhode Island Historical Society, 1988)

McLoughlin, William G. - *New England Dissent, 1630-1833: The Baptists and the Separation of Church and State.* 2 volumes. (Cambridge: Harvard University Press, 1971)

Miller, Perry - *Orthodoxy In Massachusetts, 1630-1650.* (Cambridge, MA: Harvard University Press, 1933)

Moriarty, G. A. - "The Ancestry of Dr. John Clarke of Newport, Rhode Island." *New England Historical and Genealogical Register,* (October, 1921)

Moriarty, G. A. - "The Education of Dr. John Clarke." *Rhode Island History*, vol. 15 (April, 1956)

Morison, Samuel Eliot - *The Founding of Harvard College.* (Cambridge, MA: Harvard University Press, 1935)

Nelson, Wilbur C. - *The Hero of Acquidneck: A Life of Dr. John Clarke* (New York: Fleming H. Revell, 1938)

Nelson, Wilbur C. - "Dr. John Clarke and the Baptist Beginnings in Newport." *Bulletin of the Newport Historical Society*, No. 101, (January, 1940)

James, Sydney V. - *John Clarke and His Legacies: Religion and Law in Colonial Rhode Island 1638-1750.* (University Park, PA: The Pennsylvania State University Press, 1999)

James, Sydney V. - *Colonial Rhode Island. A History.* (New York: Charles Scribner's Sons, 1975)

Sheffield, William P. - "John Clarke, Physician, Philanthropist, Preacher and Patriot." *Journal of the American Medical Association*, (August 24, 1889)

Sprague, William B. - *Annals of the American Pulpit.* Volume 6 (New York: Robert Carter & Brothers, 1865) pp. 21-26.

Stoever, William K. B. - *'A Faire and Easie Way to Heaven': Covenant Theology and Antinomianism in Early Massachusetts* (Middletown, CT: Weslyan University Press, 1978)

Whitley, W. T. - "The English Career of John Clarke, Rhode Island" *Baptist Quarterly* 1, (1922)

Wilson, Robert J. - *A Lively Experiment: The Extraordinary Career of Dr. John Clarke of Newport, Rhode Island* (Granville, MA: Pioneer Valley Baptist Association, 1983)

www.ingramcontent.com/pod-product-compliance
Lightning Source LLC
Chambersburg PA
CBHW030344030726
47499CB00003B/896